BBC
DOCTOR WHO

BBC CHILDREN'S BOOKS

UK | USA | Canada | Ireland | Australia
India | New Zealand | South Africa

BBC Children's Books are published by Puffin Books,
part of the Penguin Random House group of companies
whose addresses can be found at global.penguinrandomhouse.com.
www.penguin.co.uk www.puffin.co.uk www.ladybird.co.uk

First published 2022
Published in this edition 2023
001

Written by Faridah Àbíké-Íyímídé, Sophie Aldred, Jasbinder Bilan, Nikita Gill,
Mark Griffiths, Katy Manning, Emma Norry, Temi Oh, Sarah Daniels and Dave Rudden
Copyright © BBC, 2022

BBC and DOCTOR WHO (word marks and devices) are trade marks of the
British Broadcasting Corporation and are used under licence. BBC logo © BBC 1996.
DOCTOR WHO logo © BBC 1973. Licensed by BBC Studios.

Set in 12/19pt Baskerville MT Std
Typeset by Jouve (UK), Milton Keynes
Printed and bound in Great Britain by Clays Ltd, Elcograf S.p.A.

The authorized representative in the EEA is Penguin Random House Ireland,
Morrison Chambers, 32 Nassau Street, Dublin D02 YH68

A CIP catalogue record for this book is available from the British Library

ISBN: 978–1–405–95688–8

All correspondence to:
BBC Children's Books
Penguin Random House Children's UK
One Embassy Gardens, 8 Viaduct Gardens
London SW11 7BW

BBC
DOCTOR WHO

ORIGIN STORIES

PUFFIN

CONTENTS

CHEMISTRY

SOPHIE ALDRED

The girl with the high ponytail sat scuffing her shoes on the legs of the plastic chair outside the head's office, a familiar conversation banging around her brain.

It's not my fault . . . it was a complete accident. Why do these things always happen to me? I couldn't help it if Form Five's pottery pig collection just happened to be out on the shelf where I put my stuff. It's not fair . . .

She knew excuses or moaning would do nothing to help her already precarious position with the powers that be. So she tried to prepare a proper apology in her head, and ready herself for whatever rubbish punishment would be handed out. At least she'd had plenty of practice at fixing her face into a look of sincere contrition.

And it really hadn't been her fault this time. In fact, her experiment had been encouraged by her science teacher, who she reckoned was the only adult in the school (maybe the only adult she'd ever met, apart from her nan) who seemed to *get her*. Her teacher understood what made her tick, and why she'd want to be experimenting with chemicals in the first place.

The teacher had only joined the school a few months back. The ancient, crabby chemistry teacher, who had been there for as long as anyone could remember, and who spent lessons behind his copy of *New Scientist* (which was surely a joke, there was nothing 'new' about him), had disappeared quite suddenly – no questions asked. And the teacher who replaced him was entirely different: youngish, full of energy, asked brilliant questions which didn't seem to require sensible answers, and didn't just read out a page number in the O-level textbook and leave the class to get on with it.

Chemistry was the one and only subject that the girl actually wanted to understand, to study. Not for any stupid exam, but because of the fact that two substances could change into something else entirely when you put them together fascinated her. Everything in the whole universe, she discovered, was made up of tiny, tiny particles: atoms and molecules. Just little dots. When you broke everything down to its basic components, there was really not much there except space. That made her feel safe, somehow.

Like looking up at the stars. At least, those nights when you could actually see them through the grime and dirty cloud cover of a West London sky. It somehow made her feel small and insignificant – and that was a good thing. By comparison, the problems and anxieties (which she never admitted to anyone, not even to herself half the time) that occasionally reared up and ambushed her in the night seemed unimportant.

She had fallen in love with the periodic table the moment she turned a page and saw the different-coloured boxes, all ordered in groups, with their numbers, symbols and weights. She would pore over it, rolling the more difficult names around in her mouth, not knowing if she was pronouncing them right. She knew how to say palladium though; that was easy. It was the name of a famous theatre in the West End. When she was little, her nan had stopped smoking for weeks and saved up for two tickets to see *Aladdin* at the Palladium starring Nan's favourite bloke off the telly, Danny La Rue. They'd both shouted themselves hoarse 'HE'S BEHIND YOU!', and went home down Oxford Street on the bus in the dark, the Christmas lights twinkling overhead and the shop windows full of stuff she could only ever dream of having in her stocking.

Then there were all the obvious elements, of course: gold, silver, mercury, lead. But what about zirconium (which sounded more like a science-fiction villain – the Mysterons in *Captain Scarlet*, maybe). Or thorium (that one made her think of Norse myths). She particularly liked the sound of the planet ones, neptunium and plutonium.

She'd cut the periodic table out of her textbook and stuck it to some card with cow gum. As she covered it with sticky-backed plastic, she ran her thumb over the surface to smooth out the air bubbles, thinking about how pleased *Blue Peter* presenter Janet Ellis would be with her efforts.

She placed it proudly on her desk, and her new science teacher spotted it during the very first lesson. No one had ever admired anything she'd done before (at her school, teachers had lost the will to teach and praise, as much as the pupils had lost the urge to learn and behave) and so she started to ask the teacher tentative questions about chemistry.

Her friends were puzzled at first. Midge took the mick, and Shreela did a lot of eye-rolling and shrugging. But she didn't care. Someone she quite liked had information she was actually interested in, admired her work and, what's more, seemed to show an interest in teaching her something rather than telling her off. She found herself hanging around the lab during breaks, getting answers to her many questions. She was shocked to find she actually enjoyed spending time with a teacher, of all people.

And this teacher had more energy than anyone she'd ever met: running about the lab, pulling out books, jabbing fingers at relevant paragraphs, rushing over to the store cupboard and bringing various pots and beakers to the bench. And talking. By golly, there was lots of talking. Strange stories (some of them even nearly made sense) and all of it fascinating, thrilling, exciting. Together they wrote equations, the teacher conjuring numbers and letters out of the air and putting them together to form magic formulae. They'd turn these into substances that would transform before her eyes, with smells both good and bad, and colours and flashes brighter than anything she'd seen before.

But best of all was the day when she had worked out a brand-new recipe for a rather effective explosive, based on nitrogen. By herself.

And once she'd come up with the recipe, her teacher had given her a history lesson! With all sorts of warnings and mutterings about responsibility and codes of honour. Yes, she did know about Guy Fawkes and the trouble he got into (although she was a bit confused when the teacher started describing Guy as an 'all right bloke, really'). And yes, although she wasn't the biggest fan of Maggie Thatcher, she had been shocked when that hotel in Brighton had been blown up a few years back.

She promised her teacher – cross her heart and hope to die – that she would never use this explosive new knowledge for destructive purposes. That she would certainly never tell anyone about it, and that she would most definitely not make the recipe at home. If only the teacher had spotted that this last promise was made with her fingers firmly crossed behind her back.

She could hardly wait for the buzzer signalling the end of lessons that day, and ran all the way home to the flat, not even waiting for Midge, Shreela, Derek and the rest of the gang.

The container would have to be metal and it would have to look cool.

She searched the kitchen and eventually found what she was looking for at the back of the fridge: a squirty cream canister left over from Nan's birthday, when they were being posh and had trifle. In her bedroom she took out her penknife and started scratching off all the outer plastic covering – the logos, the pictures of cows. After a lot of careful scraping she was soon left with what could only be described as a wicked-looking can.

She took goggles and gloves from her school bag, and extracted the recipe ingredients, being super careful to keep them separate. She was pleased with herself that she'd nicked all this from under the teacher's nose . . . but then she felt an uncomfortable sensation, one she wasn't used to. She remembered that the chemistry teacher was the only adult, other than her nan, whose opinion she valued and for whom (it dawned on her suddenly) she'd do anything.

But she had crossed her fingers, after all.

Though her bedroom was a tip, she knew exactly where everything was, from the festering T-shirts strewn across the floor, down to the three mouldy coffee cups lurking under her bed. She swiped a pile of stuff off her bedside table, carefully placed the chemicals on top and gingerly measured and decanted everything into the can. She would have to do some careful research on fuses and a timing device but, for now, this would do.

She picked up one of the T-shirts from its place on the floor, wrapped it carefully round the can, and then slipped it back into her school bag. There. All done and no mishaps. Tomorrow, at school, she would find a place to stash the can so she could work on the timer at her leisure. Now there was just enough time to run up to the youth club and see who was around before Nan came over and the evening was taken up with tea and *Corrie.*

She changed out of her school uniform and grabbed her signature jacket from the back of the bedroom door. That black puffy flight jacket was her pride and joy. She'd saved up enough money from her horrible paper round to buy it from Millets . . . and then started collecting badges, safety pins and other cool things to decorate it with. She'd got the idea from a very trendy magazine, spotted while she'd been collecting the papers from the cruddy newsagent. She'd never seen a magazine like that before and had spent several minutes flicking through the pages. It was a door into another world – one where she could only dream of belonging. There were so many bands, most of which she'd never heard of, and photos of so many beautiful people: girls out clubbing, wearing these puffy jackets, baseball caps and cycling shorts. She thought perhaps she could try recreating the look, even if she could never be in a cool band or go to expensive clubs. Then annoying Mr Corner Shop had shouted at her to get her grubby paws off the mags and get on with her job. She'd rolled her eyes, tutted, picked up her heavy paper-round bag and flounced out of the door.

But since then she'd done her best, on a limited budget, to emulate those girls. Yes, she got some looks from the gang at first, but she could tell that, secretly, they thought she looked wicked.

When she got to the club it was deserted. The gang must have gone to the mouldy old shopping precinct to eat chips and hang out. Well, she couldn't be bothered with that this evening. She walked on up the hill, past all the scrappy places where people dumped crisp packets and empty cider bottles. Only slightly out of breath, she stood at the top. The sparse trees were jagged and black, their twisty shapes silhouetted against the darkening winter sky. Down below, the lights were just beginning to come on in the estates, and out along Western Avenue, illuminating the road as it snaked out of London towards the new motorway that had just been built to circle right round the city. She hadn't been up here for ages. It was actually quite beautiful, in its way.

Then something down near the road bridge caught her eye. Squinting in the gloom, she spotted something she'd never noticed before. It looked like a blue version of a phone box, with a light on top that was flashing on and off. How odd. She'd been that way hundreds of times when she went to visit her mate Derek, who lived on the other side of the A40 (the posh bit near the golf course). She made up her mind to go and take a look before tea – there would be just enough time before Nan started to worry.

Scrambling back down the path in the gathering gloom, a thought struck her. She should really come clean about that whole 'fingers behind the back' thing with the science teacher. Her face suddenly felt hot, and her stomach clenched uncomfortably. This was a new and unusual sensation. Usually she was quite happy to be 'economical with the truth' (as that politician had so tricksily put it). It basically meant lying, but now all the kids at school were saying it as it sounded so much cleverer than 'I lied'.

But there was something different about lying to an adult who you respected and admired, and who had actually gone out of their way to give you a helping hand in life. Well, tomorrow, she'd put that right. She would go straight to the lab (the teacher seemed to prefer hanging out there to sitting in the staffroom) and make a heartfelt and genuine apology and hand over the can.

On she went, feeling slightly relieved. Past the houses, through the playground (giving the obligatory push to the roundabout as she went) and across the playing field towards the bridge. But when she arrived, there was just the same old graffitied bit of wall, the bin surrounded by rubbish . . . and no sign of the blue phone box. Strange. She had good eyesight and was pretty sure about what she'd seen. She'd ask Derek at school tomorrow; he might know something.

Now it really was getting dark, so she turned back and hurried home by the light of the street lamps.

After a fitful night's sleep and no breakfast (the milk had gone off and there was no bread) she hurried to school to make her 'confession'. Arriving outside the lab, she double-checked her bag for the carefully wrapped can. Having spent the night justifying her actions to herself, her new plan was to hand it over with a winning grin, say 'Pressie for you!' and saunter off to assembly, no questions asked. It was funny how, now it came to it, she didn't really want to make a big fuss of things, after all.

However, best-laid plans and all that.

When she got to the lab, she pressed her nose against the square of safety glass in the door and peered left and right. Usually, the teacher would be leaping around the room, muttering and gesticulating to no one at all, stopping to write frantic notes in a scrappy book grabbed from a seemingly bottomless pocket. Then, when she'd spotted her at the door, waving her in to show her some new find or an amazing equation. But, to her dismay, there emerged from the storeroom a grizzled, stout figure in a shabby lab coat holding a pile of dog-eared textbooks, which he started distributing ever so slowly among the lab benches. Of her beloved teacher there was no sign.

So she would have to put up with a supply teacher reading from the textbook. Boring, boring, same old, same old. It felt as if someone had taken the stuffing out of her and she groaned out loud.

Then she remembered the can.

As the day went on, she realised there was no way she could put it back. The old supply teacher might seem doddery, but he had eyes like a hawk and rarely left the lab. She hurried along there in her lunch break to find him sitting, spotted handkerchief tucked into his collar as a napkin, Tupperware box open on the desk in front of him, munching through what smelled like tuna sandwiches. She beat a hasty retreat.

She couldn't take the can home, either, because she really had no idea if it was safe – and if it *was* going to go off then (a) school would be the best place for an explosion and (b) it couldn't be traced back to her.

The gang were beginning to wonder why she hadn't put her bag down all day. She even took it to the dining hall for the nasty stew that was served up as lunch (along with something passing for mash, plonked on to the plate with an

ice-cream scoop). Midge started teasing her, until good old
Shreela stepped in, sensing there was something secret going
on and that her best chance of being in on it would be to
back up her friend. She took Midge aside and started
whispering loudly. Something about 'time of the month',
'endometriosis', and finally 'back off, you idiot'. Midge went a
lovely shade of lobster and promptly backed off.

Double art after lunch provided an opportunity at
last. Mrs Parkinson did a great impression of a hippy art
teacher, in her saggy dungarees and swathes of headscarves.
Until there was any *hint* of trouble. Then she turned into a
raptor. Luckily, it was lino-cutting that afternoon. So there
was a diversion when Sticky Luke managed to gouge out a
sizeable chunk of thumb, having made the rookie lino-cutter's
mistake of putting his hand in front of the blade instead of
behind it. As Mrs Parkinson spent many minutes holding
Luke's bleeding hand up in the air (to stop the bleeding)
and berating the whole class for not listening to her safety
warnings, the girl saw her moment. Reaching into her bag,
she gingerly eased the T-shirt-wrapped canister up and out
and slipped it on to a shelf behind some lumpy, recently
glazed clay objects (so ugly and misshapen that no one would
be taking them home to show Mum any time soon). Her plan
was to come back the following week when, she hoped, the

proper science teacher would be back from being ill or away or whatever was the problem, and deal with it then.

But next week came, and the supply teacher was still there, and no one seemed to know what was happening. When she asked Einstein (as they had newly nicknamed the supply teacher) he said it was none of her business and to get back to page fifty-four. No amount of scowling seemed to make any difference.

And then the following week the art room blew up.

Well, that was an exaggeration, but it had made a pretty good bang. The misshapen clay lumps had turned out to be Form Five's prized pottery pig collection (who knew?). Fortunately, no one had been in the art room at the time of the explosion. Unfortunately for her, large pieces of her easily identifiable T-shirt had been strewn around, along with lumps of pig.

The worst thing was that no one had really said anything to her at the time. A letter had been sent home (that had been easy enough to intercept) and there were mutterings of police involvement. But that hadn't led to anything, luckily, and she thought she'd got away with it. Yet here she was, waiting for the inevitable Big Trouble she was undoubtedly in.

'Dorothy!'

The headmaster's voice made her jump. And wince. How she hated that name. She stopped kicking the chair legs, put on her best 'I'm ashamed of what I did and I'll never do it again' face, pulled up her socks, adjusted her school tie to normal and opened the door.

He sat behind the large imposing desk, eyes lowered, tapping a pen, slowly and annoyingly, on a large old book in front of him.

'So. Dorothy. Again. What do you have to say for yourself this time?'

'I'm sorry, sir. I can guarantee that it will never happen again. It was an accident and I didn't mean to do it.'

He put down the pen – painfully slowly – his gaze still lowered.

'Well, well. What are we going to do with you? It seems you just cannot be trusted. This . . . creation of yours. What do you call it?'

'Nitro 9, sir.'

'Yes, most ingenious. And you really came up with it all by yourself?'

A pause. And now she too lowered her gaze, giving herself time to think. If she said anything about the science teacher's help, it would be curtains for them both.

'Well, that tells me a lot. About you. Loyal, bright, trustworthy up to a point.'

A look of confusion mixed with a certain amount of surprise spread across her face. What the heck was this about? She'd expected the usual 'don't do it again, hundreds of lines to write out, staying in at break for the next year' routine.

'How about you tell me everything you know about your science teacher? And if the information proves useful, we might be able to come to . . . some arrangement, that doesn't involve further investigation.'

She took in a sharp breath.

She would never agree to tell on the teacher. And yet, it was such an easy way of getting off scot-free . . .

'I'm sorry, Mr Michaels, I'm not sure what you mean. The teacher was in the lab with me the whole time and was really good at health and safety. Everything I did, I did myself. It was all my fault. I worked it all out and made it and I'm sorry I nicked the chemicals and I'll pay for all the damage and . . .' She trailed off, realising Mr Michaels wasn't the slightest bit interested in what she was saying.

And it was at that moment, as she at last raised her eyes to his, that she realised there was something really weird going on. The knot in her stomach turned into a less definable sensation. Surprised, she guessed this must be the rarely felt emotion (for her, at least) of *fear*.

For the man, if indeed it was a man, sitting in front of her and doing his best Mr Michaels impersonation, was not the world-weary, slightly dog-eared headmaster of countless boring assemblies and many tellings-off. It was something her brain couldn't quite twist itself around. For a start, Mr Michaels, unless she had missed something, did not normally have scary shiny red eyes and puffy cheeks that were getting puffier by the second.

He, or rather it (the resemblance to a human being was now distinctly shaky), slammed what looked like giant paws – with claws beginning to sprout from them – hard on the desk as he rose out of the chair. The cheap nylon suit and tie once inhabited by the hapless Mr Michaels began to rip and tear as the body inside it grew and morphed and transmogrified into . . . Well, the girl had no idea what it was. She stood frozen to the spot, at once scared yet strangely fascinated to see what would happen next. The creature (all vestiges of Mr Michaels had disappeared) raised its . . . what? Front legs? Arms? Tentacles? A great howling wind started whipping around the office, gathering up papers, books, pens and pencils and whirling them into a mini tornado. She watched transfixed as the whirlwind came towards her, not knowing what to do and unable to move as the creature's red eyes seemed to pin her to the spot.

There was a sudden bang behind her, which broke the spell, and she turned her head. There, framed in the doorway, was a familiar figure, long grey-blue coat flapping, boots planted firmly on the ground, arms braced against the door frame, blond bob blown about by the wind.

'ACE! WHEN I SAY RUN, RUN!' she shouted into the tornado . . . 'RUUUN!'

Ace didn't need any more prompting. The creature had now grown almost as tall as the ceiling and the tornado was getting larger and more furious, as though it was about to whip her up into it. She darted towards the door, struggling against the swirl of the wind pulling at her heels. The science teacher held out a hand which Ace caught, and she was dragged into the corridor, just as the teacher threw something from one of her bottomless pockets into the room, before slamming the door behind them.

There was a sizzling sound and then a pop and then all went quiet.

'And that, my dear Ace, is the end of that!' The teacher beamed, her brown eyes twinkling.

'What the heck?' said Ace. 'End of what, exactly?'

'Although, strictly speaking,' the teacher went on, 'it's actually the beginning. Of everything. Of the future you. Or is it the past? It's so confusing sometimes. Time is a many-splendoured thing when you really stop and take a look.'

'But hang on, what about that . . . thing in there? And the wind and everything? And what's happened to Mr Michaels?'

The teacher took a deep breath. 'Last things first. Thirdly, Mr Michaels is right now boring the socks off Class 7B with a general knowledge quiz. Secondly, the wind and stuff was a mini time storm conjured up by an old acquaintance of mine and easily got rid of by the temporal retrorsus manipulator I threw at it (I knew that would come in handy one day). And firstly, that poor creature was definitely nothing to do with Mr Michaels – though it was using a clone of his body which must have been very uncomfy; tight and itchy, I imagine, for a Charvalian . . .'

She paused for breath. Ace's mouth remained open but of words there was no sign.

'Anyway. You don't need to worry about any of it. Your bit happens later; we're not quite ready for you yet. Or me, come to think of it. Well, me as I am now. It's complicated.'

'You're telling me . . .' Ace croaked.

'Thing is, Ace,' continued the teacher, getting more serious now and putting both hands firmly on Ace's shoulders, 'you will have a part to play, a very important part. And although I have to go now, I promise you, cross my hearts and hope to die, we will meet again. It won't be me . . . well, it will be, but you won't see this particular me till you're really quite old. Old compared to now, I mean, not old old, but you know what I mean . . .'

'I have no idea what you mean!' exclaimed Ace. 'You are making no sense and I don't understand any of it.'

The teacher smiled kindly into Ace's eyes and suddenly looked very ancient, very wise and very tired.

'I have to go now,' she sighed, 'and you won't be seeing me here again. But I want you to promise me that you will stay as brilliant as you are, always ask questions, always go for it. Because you are an ace human being and you are going to have a life beyond your wildest dreams. Now, I'm so sorry I have to do this. You're not going to remember any of this, but there is a really good reason and it will all work out in the end. It always does.'

As Ace opened her mouth to remonstrate, the teacher swiftly placed her hands on either side of Ace's head, and all at once she felt a warm peace running through her whole

body, rather like drinking hot chocolate on a frosty day . . .
but even better.

And suddenly there she was, standing in the empty corridor
outside Mr Michaels' office, wondering what on earth she
was doing.

From the end of the corridor came a shout.

'Ace! There you are! We've been looking everywhere for
you. Manesha thought you must have bunked off gym cos of
your "you know what", but you weren't in the sick room . . .'

Derek chattered on as they walked together back to the
classroom block.

'Fancy coming to the club tonight? There's a new bloke
in charge, apparently, and he's doing some self-defence stuff.
Doesn't sound too shabby.'

There was something nagging in the back of Ace's brain.
Something she had been meaning to ask Derek, but she
couldn't for the life of her remember what it was.

'Sure,' she replied, 'don't see why not. After all, a girl's
got to be prepared for anything these days.'

MY DADDY
FIGHTS
MONSTERS

DAVE RUDDEN

You can always rely on Kate Lethbridge-Stewart to brighten up *class presentations*, Mrs Lafferty thought, leaning back in her chair and folding her arms.

'Very good, Kate,' she said. 'Tell us more.'

It was 2 p.m. on what felt like the eighth Monday of June, and the sun was oozing through the window like treacle, turning the young minds of 4A soft and warm and easily distractable. And because the pupils had stopped listening to Mrs Lafferty in May, but still occasionally listened to each other, she had decided to have them give presentations on Daddy's Job.

'Um . . .'

Kate Lethbridge-Stewart was small and slender and blonde. You might have described her as elfin, though traditionally elves didn't have black eyes from fighting boys in 5B. Apparently, the boy had asked why Kate's dad had left. Mrs Lafferty had no idea how he'd found out, but news in St Agnes, and Pinswick in general, travelled fast.

According to the teacher who had found them, Kate hadn't shown the slightest bit of hesitation in taking on someone twice her size. Now, standing in front of twenty of her peers, she had gone the colour of old milk.

It made Mrs Lafferty that little bit more determined to encourage her.

'Go on, Kate.'

The little girl's words all came out in a rush, like a cork had been pulled.

'My dad is a brigadier and that's a really high-up rank and he works for UNIT that's the United Nations Intelligence Taskforce and that's supposed to be a secret but I saw it in a letter once that he forgot to put in his safe and we've moved here for a little bit because he's away and when I asked my mummy what he was doing she said fighting monsters.'

'Didn't know we were allowed to just make stuff up,' Billy Ryan said sourly from the back of the room, before Mrs Lafferty shot him a look that made his teeth clack shut.

'That's very interesting, Kate,' she said. 'And what kind of monsters does your daddy fight?'

Kate thought for a moment.

'Big ones.'

'Very good, Kate,' Mrs Lafferty said. 'Now, sit down and we'll hear from –'

'Big hairy ones with teeth,' Kate said firmly. 'And slimy ones with lots of arms. And . . . and . . .'

She looked around the classroom, her expression a little wild. Mrs Lafferty was used to that look. You saw it all the time, when pupils hadn't done the reading and instead decided just to start talking in the hope they'd begin making sense halfway through.

It was sad to see someone scramble for details about their own father.

'*I* could just have made something up,' Billy Ryan said, and Gerald Thimbley sniggered.

'I've read your English homework, Billy,' Mrs Lafferty said smoothly, 'and we both know that's not true.'

The pug-headed little boy scowled. Mrs Lafferty had met Billy's father at parent–teacher meetings. They had been an . . . experience. She had done her own presentation on the experience afterwards to her husband that evening.

'Axons!' Kate said suddenly. The whole class turned back to look at her. Then her voice went very small. 'I heard him on the phone once. He fought Axons.'

'*Thank you*, Kate,' Mrs Lafferty said firmly. It sounded like a good monster name at least. Some of the things the children came out with were truly awful. 'Next!'

The Assessor masquerading as Billy Ryan let itself in the front door and, with the sigh of someone kicking off uncomfortable work shoes, dropped its school bag and unzipped the front of its skull.

'Finally.'

The Assessor's name was Crinix B-Theta, and inside its false-flesh disguise it was long and spindly and segmented, like a dentist's tool designed for a scorpion. The *real* Billy Ryan, along with his family, was lying asleep on the floor, and for a moment Crinix B-Theta thought about waking them up to share the good news.

Last time it had tried that, however, all they had done was scream, and so Crinix B-Theta had to put them to sleep again. That was fine. Assessors were used to talking to themselves.

Earth was challenging. Every Assessor knew it. There were far better assignments in the galaxy. Assignments Assessors would kill for, and frequently did. When you were a species of spies and data brokers, what mattered was being close to information and influence. Sontar, Dyastoborum, the asteroid home of the Shadow Proclamation – these were areas of importance, planets around which the universe turned, and every single one of them had an Assessor undercover there, quietly taking notes.

And then there was Earth – an insipid little dirtball with a Level Five civilisation and no notion of the vast and vibrant universe above their heads. It was a desperately uninteresting place, and the only thing that put it on the stellar map was the fact that for some reason a Time Lord of Gallifrey seemed to visit at least once a week.

Crinix B-Theta stretched to its full length, trying to work the ache out of each crooked pincer and spine. It had seemed like such a smart idea to come here, at first. Information about Time Lords – their capabilities, their technology, their motivations – was gold on the data market. You could sell it three or four times over, to Daleks and Rutans and sometimes even other Time Lords. Because nobody trusted Time Lords, least of all Time Lords themselves.

But you had to be careful. Very careful. Observing the Doctor in their natural habitat was out, for obvious reasons – no Assessor who had tried to infiltrate Gallifrey had ever returned. And observing them in the wild was almost impossible because they were the very definition of a moving target.

So Crinix B-Theta watched the people they knew, and the places they liked, and did it all in secret, which was difficult, because Time Lords had senses not even Assessors could fool.

It was risky. It was dangerous. And Crinix B-Theta had been just about ready to cross Kate Stewart off its list. She didn't know the first thing about UNIT, or the Doctor. Her father the Brigadier had seemed to keep it that way on purpose.

Until today.

'Very good, Kate,' the Assessor repeated, in a perfect imitation of Mrs Lafferty's voice. 'Tell us more.'

Fiona Lethbridge-Stewart had her armour of cheeriness in place before Kate's key had finished turning in the door.

Maybe today she won't slam it.

'I'm making biscuits!' Fiona called. 'Come and try one!'

Slam.

It had been three months. Military campaigns had not lasted as long. And Fiona had heard Kate come home angry enough times in that month that she knew the frustrated melody of her daughter's arrival like a favourite song, but still she turned the sink tap off and listened. There was always a chance. Always a hope that there might be some minor variation. That's what you did when your only daughter was angry at you. You hoped.

She'll fling the bag down, Fiona thought, a second before the dry slap of canvas echoed from the hall.

The keys. A grumpy jangle into the cup on the side table.

And the coat. Keys and bags were one thing, but it took real talent to hang up a coat angrily.

'What did you do today at school, love?'

Kate burst into the little kitchen like a thistledown storm, shoes squeaking on the worn tiles. They'd stayed with Fiona's parents in Chichester after the separation. It had been a godsend, until it hadn't. There were only so many times one could listen to your mother suggest that maybe actually your marriage was fine and you were being too demanding.

So, they had gone to Uncle Reggie's house, which had been empty since his passing. It was small, and the doors stuck, and there were paint cans everywhere from the freshening-up Reggie had never got around to starting. It wasn't what anyone would call child-suitable, not least because Reggie had served in the war and brought home quite a lot of souvenirs. But at least it was just them, and that would make it easier for Fiona and Kate to talk.

Just as soon as I figure out what I'm going to say.

'Ah!' Fiona said, neatly catching Kate's wrist before she could grab a biscuit. 'No treats without conversation, I'm afraid.'

Kate scowled at her, but the warm smell of biscuits was evidently irresistible. Which was precisely why Fiona had baked them. Biscuits bought her conversation. Nothing she had done so far had won her a smile.

'Your eye is looking better.'

The school had called to tell Fiona what happened. Apparently, the other boy looked much worse, which should not have pleased Fiona as much as it did.

Kate stuck out her lower lip.

'Did Daddy call?'

'No,' Fiona said. 'I said I'd tell you if he does, didn't I? Daddy is very busy with work. That's why we're here in Pinswick. To give Daddy space to do his work.'

Don't say it. Don't say it, Fiona urged herself.

'Just for a little while.'

Coward.

'How long is a little while?' Kate asked sullenly, as she had every day since they'd left.

Fiona didn't have an answer. That was the thing about being a parent. You were, as an adult, supposed to have answers. You were supposed to be rational and logical and do the right and wise thing. Presumably that was why you were the one in charge.

Unfortunately, all being a parent taught you was that actually it was children who were the rational ones. There was a reason behind everything a child did. They complained when they were hungry; they got grumpy when they were tired.

Adults, however, were a mess of conflicting emotions and motivations and expectations. It was adults who made choices without understanding them, who said hurtful things without meaning them, who found themselves angry because of the past and the future and missed dinners and forgotten birthdays and a vague sense that *this was not how it was supposed to be*. Except that it had always been like that, so what did she expect?

I felt like I was married to a state funeral waiting to happen.

I felt like I was alone when I had been promised a life together.

How did you explain all that to a child, when Fiona could barely explain it to herself?

Kate was still looking at her with that ferocious, angry curiosity. Children needed reasons. It helped them make sense of things. And, at first, they had helped Fiona too. She'd always told Kate her daddy was out fighting and being brave, and as those big hungry eyes had stared at her, the stories had to become bigger and bigger to fill them.

It wasn't lying. That was what Fiona had told herself. She didn't *know* what Alistair did. He'd never told her. Official Secrets Act and all that. *How can it be lying if I don't know what the truth is?*

So Fiona made up exciting adventures for Kate about Alistair that tried to explain why he was never home, and Kate had clung to them as any child would, and now, in the absence of Fiona actually biting the bullet and telling her daughter the truth of their separation, those stories were all Kate had.

'Well?' Kate said, eyes narrowing.

'You're very like him, you know,' Fiona said, because it was easier than saying anything else. 'Very determined. He wouldn't let go of things either.'

Kate's voice was very solemn.

'Does that mean you're going to stop liking me too?'

Tears suddenly pricked Fiona's eyes.

'Kate! I would never –'

But someone was knocking at the door, and Kate had already pulled away.

Outside the door, Crinix B-Theta adjusted its dress and gave its Mrs Lafferty disguise a once-over in a pocket mirror. *Perfect.* Mimicking Billy Ryan had been easy. No one really paid attention to children. Mrs Lafferty, however, was a public figure in this little town. At any moment on the walk here someone might have stopped Crinix B-Theta and asked about exam results or school policy or any one of a hundred details that might give the Assessor away.

Of course, if anything like that happened, Crinix B-Theta had some tricks to fall back on. Assessors weren't capable of grand psychic feats, unfortunately. Not for them the total cloaking of the Silence, or the shapeshifting of the Multi-form. *Not strong, but highly tuned.* That was what they said at the Academy. Crinix B-Theta had been top of its class, and all it could really manage was a little memory manipulation, some illusion work, and the occasional psychic nudge to send someone to sleep or make them cooperate.

It didn't think that would be needed with Kate. She was dying to boast about her father to anyone who would listen. Crinix B-Theta had been ready to dismiss it all as fairy tales until the little girl had mentioned Axons. What else had Kate overheard? What secrets might she carry about UNIT and its mysterious scientific advisor?

And, more importantly, what might interested parties pay for them?

Crinix B-Theta knocked again, noting the peeling paint on the doorframe and the garden struggling with weeds.

Every other house on the street was beautifully kept, not a blade of grass out of place. A few doors down, a child leaving their home with their mother blanched as it saw that strangest of all things – a teacher outside of school – and Crinix B-Theta indulged itself by twisting Mrs Lafferty's face into a wicked smile.

In this line of work, it was the little things.

You were sensitive to knocks on the door, as an army wife.

It wasn't that Fiona thought it was Alistair. His knock was brisk. Not impolite, certainly, but with the quiet strength of someone who knew that their business was important. There were probably courses about it.

But mingled with that new relief was old fear. The fear that it was one of his superiors. The fear that it was the news so many army wives got, the news that made them army widows instead.

'Daddy?'

Kate was different, of course. She wasn't as used to Alistair's knock because he usually came home after she'd gone to sleep, or maybe she just wanted it to be him so much that she didn't care. She barrelled down the hallway and flung open the door without so much as a moment's hesitation.

'Pet,' Fiona said. 'Wait –'

'Hello,' said Mrs Lafferty. 'Parent–teacher meeting.'

'This is . . . unusual,' Fiona Lethbridge-Stewart said, and Crinix B-Theta could only agree.

A lot of effort had gone into the Assessor's Mrs Lafferty disguise, but Crinix B-Theta was proud of the finished result. Weeks of lurking behind Billy Ryan's face had given the Assessor plenty of opportunity to make a study of the teacher – all the little micro-expressions and messiness that made a human a human.

Mrs Lafferty was *fun* to be. She glared a lot. She rolled her eyes when people were being inefficient, and thought she was good at hiding it, which she wasn't. People were *afraid* of her. It was a delight.

And yet, Fiona Lethbridge-Stewart did not seem cowed. She didn't appear happy, either. She didn't invite the Assessor in, but instead stepped out on to the tired-looking porch, saying something inaudible to Kate and then shutting her inside.

'We just wanted to check up on Kate,' the Assessor said. Parents liked it when you cared. 'Make sure she's all right after the . . . incident.'

'Will you be speaking to the other child's parents?' Fiona asked, scowling as if she already knew the answer. 'Kate shouldn't be blamed for any of it. I don't care that she broke his nose. It was –'

'Impressive,' the Assessor said, smiling with Mrs Lafferty's mouth. After a moment, Fiona smiled too.

'Thank you for coming out. It's very kind of you.'

'Not at all. May I . . . speak to her?'

Fiona frowned, and Crinix B-Theta briefly considered giving her a little mental nudge. You had to be careful. It took real psychic muscle to make someone do something they truly did not want to do. Better to finesse it. Wait until you found something they wanted to do and help them along.

'Yes, of course,' Fiona said eventually. 'Let me go and get her.'

No invitation in. Suspicious, or embarrassed about her home? Humans were funny about such things.

'Of course,' Crinix B-Theta said, and stepped back to wait.

Fiona disappeared inside, closing the door behind her. A minute passed, then two, and the Assessor began to feel the first stirrings of unease pull at its antennae. You didn't spend years as a deep-cover agent without learning to trust your instincts, and something here wasn't right.

The street was empty. The June sunlight didn't quite reach through the trees, and the neglected porch of the

Lethbridge-Stewarts' house was unexpectedly cold. Wind raked the hedges. A dog was whining somewhere, high and shrill and angry, and though the false-flesh of Mrs Lafferty was designed with multiple breathing holes and ventilation grilles, the Assessor felt breathless with anxiety all the same.

They know.

The one thing Assessors did better than spy was gossip, and there were a thousand stories of that last big score, that crumb of priceless data that, if sold, would set you up for life. You were never more vulnerable, the superstition went, than during that last day. There was never a bigger chance that things might go wrong.

Perhaps the Brigadier was inside, loading a pistol. Perhaps a squad of UNIT soldiers were even now creeping up through next door's garden, rifles raised. Maybe the Time Lord – that great and terrible elder being, that grim old monster of the cosmos – was about to drop down from the fourth dimension and turn Crinix B-Theta into a smear on their boot.

It was suddenly very hard to breathe. The Assessor had racked up whole weeks folded away in smaller spaces than this, but suddenly it felt flabby and squashed, as if it had accidentally covered the ventilation holes and was suffocating inside its own disguise.

You got greedy, this close to a big score. You got careless. And there were urges, wild urges, that came with undercover work. Every Assessor knew it. They would sneak up on you when you were close to something good, or just through something bad. When a mission had gone sour. When a success was close enough to taste.

The Assessor felt it now – a tight and sickly pinch.

Reveal yourself.

Insanity.

You're going to suffocate in this thing.

Ludicrousness.

A breath. That's all. Clear your head.

And, just like that, Crinix B-Theta's fingers were at the secret clasp behind the false-flesh disguise's ear.

Mrs Lafferty's face unzipped, and then Fiona Lethbridge-Stewart opened the door.

Some time later, Fiona would be quite proud that she hadn't screamed.

Finding Mrs Lafferty at her door had been quite the shock in the first place. The teacher had eyes like Alistair – quiet, contemplative. Fiona had informed her of the separation – Kate had already been misbehaving when they arrived in Pinswick – and Mrs Lafferty hadn't offered

sympathy, because it had been quite obvious Fiona didn't
want it.

The teacher had just nodded, and said she'd keep an eye
on the girl as much as she could.

'Oh,' clacked a pair of chitinous jaws now protruding
from the scooped-out bowl of Mrs Lafferty's head, its beady
eyes wide and bright. The voice was unmistakably that of Mrs
Lafferty, except that it was clearly coming from between the
insect's mandibles rather than the woman's mouth. 'Oh *dear*.'

Fiona slammed the door in both its faces and spun
round. Kate was staring up at her with saucer eyes.

'*You just slammed the door in a teacher's face*,' she whispered.
Despite the horror, it was almost painfully good to see a
shocked little smile on her daughter's mouth.

And then the full bulk of Mrs Lafferty slammed into the
door behind them.

'I just need a second of your time!'

Fiona picked up Kate and ran.

'Where are we going? What's *happening*?'

Fiona didn't have a good answer for that question either.
She had Kate under one arm, squirming and wriggling, and
reached the back door *just* as she remembered that the back
door hadn't opened since Uncle Reggie had hair.

Think, Fiona. Be . . . be tactical.

What in the name of God was *that thing?*

A prank. A hallucination. A bad, waking dream.

Fiona was suddenly hit by a memory – she and Alistair in their sitting room, late at night after she'd drunk three glasses of wine and he hadn't had any because it was one of those long weeks where he seemed anywhere but in their marriage.

She had asked him point blank.

What do you do at work?

And he hadn't answered. Of course. The solid, redoubtable Brigadier. The rules weren't *rules* for Alistair. They were physics. He could no more break them than he could fly.

He had just looked at her, and in that look she had some sort of answer.

Knowledge was power, but it was also pain. Fiona knew that for a fact.

A horrible thought occurred to her, as the front door splintered and shook.

'Kate,' she said with horror. 'What did you do today at school?'

There were Assessors who controlled armies. There were Assessors who commanded battleships that could burn this world to ash. There were Assessors whose false-flesh disguises emulated the most dangerous creatures in the universe. And, of course, there was the Grand High Assessor, who was so powerful it did not wear a disguise at all.

And then there was Crinix B-Theta, in the body of a stocky teacher from Batsford, who had just broken its shoulder trying to smash in a door.

When I sell whatever Kate Stewart knows, I am treating myself to a deluxe model.

It charged one more time, and finally the hinges gave. The door fell with a clatter, and Crinix B-Theta staggered into the house, trying to fit the crushed and dangling arm back into its socket. Really, this was all incredibly embarrassing.

Now, where are they –

A paint can hit it in the face. The blow might have killed a regular human. As it was, Crinix B-Theta was rattled around like a bean in a jar. Mrs Lafferty's false face, unzipped in a moment of weakness the Assessor still could not explain, nearly came away entirely.

And Fiona Lethbridge-Stewart barrelled past it, carrying Kate, and bolted for the stairs.

'Come *back*,' Crinix B-Theta snarled, accompanying the words with a pulse of psychic demand. It nearly worked, too – the woman stopped halfway up the stairs, swaying as the mind-hold took. But then Kate wailed in her arms, and there wasn't a psychic in the galaxy that could silence the desperate parental urge to make a scream like that stop.

Fiona stooped, and Crinix B-Theta had to throw itself backwards to avoid another can of Magnolia White taking its head off entirely. By the time it had righted itself, senses still off-kilter, the two humans had vanished upstairs. Not for the first time, it wished that Assessors carried weapons. But that was the thing – they weren't soldiers, they were spies. Being a spy meant being unseen. If you had to draw a weapon, you were doing it wrong.

That anxiety surfaced again – rising up around it like boiling steam. Crinix B-Theta had to fight through it to move.

What is that? What was that worming doubt, that terror squeezing its mind?

And then Crinix B-Theta understood.

And knew what it had to do.

Kate didn't ask any questions as Fiona flung her on to Uncle Reggie's bed. That's how she knew her daughter was truly frightened.

'One second, darling,' Fiona said with manic cheer, 'I just need to find something.'

Uncle Reggie. Uncle Reggie who sang far too loudly at family birthdays and told inappropriate war stories and had once sat with Alistair for a long time in the garden and then firmly told Fiona that she had found 'one of the good ones, even if he was of the officer class'.

Reggie who kept souvenirs.

She flung herself to her knees in front of Reggie's cheap old wardrobe and rummaged through the black bags and yellowing shirts folded on top.

'Mama?'

Kate hadn't called Fiona *Mama* in years.

'Get under the bed, Kate,' Fiona said. 'Now. I'll explain in just a little bit.'

There. An old tin box, the kind you put tea or biscuits in, and the pistol inside, gleaming like new.

'Fiona?'

The voice was soft. Hesitant. And when she heard it Fiona Lethbridge-Stewart went so cold the butt of the pistol felt warm in her palm.

'Fiona, are you in the bedroom?'

It was Alistair.

The anxiety had been the answer, of course.

Crinix B-Theta should have figured it out sooner. Assessors were psychic. *Not strong but highly tuned.* And Crinix B-Theta had come here, to a house where two people were struggling, with absence and presence and each other and themselves, and Crinix B-Theta had walked right into it like a Geiger counter into a uranium mine.

But now that anxiety was going to work for it.

Psychic manipulation was easiest when the subject wanted to believe what you were telling them. When they wanted to do it anyway. Then you weren't fighting them. You were helping them along. And wouldn't these two both be relieved that the brave Brigadier had come home to protect them?

'Fiona? Kate?' Crinix B-Theta said again, with the voice of Alistair Lethbridge-Stewart and all the psychic energy it could muster. 'Can you come down so we can talk?'

Fiona barely caught Kate before she reached the door.

'It's *Dad*!' Kate shouted, her voice almost a wail, and Fiona found herself nearly falling back on to the carpet with the force of the little girl's desperate straining. 'He's come – come to protect us, come to –'

The two of them grappled, and had Fiona not been on the floor and face to face with her daughter, she might not have seen it.

Kate's eyes weren't just Kate's. There was something else in there too.

And then Fiona felt it. A warmth, bubbling up between the folds of her brain. It was the strangest sensation – her but not her, something she knew was utterly outside herself but somehow inside her head at the same time.

Alistair was here. Things were simple again. They could go home. They could leave Pinswick, and this musty old house, and try to salvage their marriage. It would be easy. Fiona hadn't realised how much she wanted that. For things to be simple. For everything to go back to the way it was.

All she had to do was take Kate and go downstairs.

'It's going to be all right, pet,' she said, hugging Kate tight. 'Daddy's here. Everything is going to be all right.'

And Kate stiffened in her arms.

Crinix B-Theta reached the landing and made its way towards the bedroom.

The Mrs Lafferty disguise wouldn't fool anyone any more. One arm hung loose and limp. The shoulder was dented and deformed, and the false-flesh face hung by a thread, exposing the chitinous Assessor to the warm June air.

Yet none of that mattered, because every ounce of the Assessor's psychic talent was projecting warmth and trust into the heads of Fiona and Kate Lethbridge-Stewart. It didn't matter, because Crinix B-Theta was going to find out what they knew about UNIT and the Doctor, and then it was never setting foot on Earth again.

'Open the door, Fiona,' Crinix B-Theta said, in the voice of Alistair Lethbridge-Stewart. 'You poor thing. Open the door and let me look at you, my darling.'

It placed one fleshy hand on the doorknob and began to turn it, and then a gunshot removed part of the door next to its head.

Crinix B-Theta went very still.

'I'm actually quite a good shot,' Fiona said, on the other side of the door. Her voice was wary. Ground down. Like the violent events of the last few minutes were just the full stop on a long and difficult story. 'My uncle used to teach me. And he has a lot of bullets in here.'

The distant, assessing part of Crinix B-Theta's brain helpfully pointed out that, going by the discharge noise and exit crater, the weapon was old, probably World War Two era, and that Fiona was either exaggerating her skill, or her hand was shaking quite badly.

Not that it made much difference. False-flesh disguises weren't meant to be shot at, and neither was Crinix B-Theta. If having to draw a weapon was a sign you had failed in your assignment, being shot at was far worse.

'I don't want to hurt you,' Crinix B-Theta said, in its *true* voice – a dry, dead whisper. 'I was just looking for –'

'My husband?' Fiona said icily. 'We're separated.'

'Information,' Crinix B-Theta finished. 'That's all. For anything you and Kate –'

'*Don't say her name.*'

Crinix B-Theta flinched.

'For anything either of you knows about what your . . . what the Brigadier does. Who he knows. That's all. Data.' The Assessor's voice was almost a whine. 'Just data.'

A long silence, and then Kate spoke, her voice small and shaking.

'We don't know anything. I don't know anything. Just some words.'

'Kate, don't talk to it –'

'It's OK, Mama.' The little girl's voice strengthened. 'You're in our heads, aren't you? I can feel it. Pushing us. Trying to get us to believe your . . . your story.'

'Kate, how do you –'

'Monsters can do all sorts of things,' Kate said, with the calm acceptance of a child. 'And if it's in our heads, it should be able to see I'm telling the truth. Monster?'

'Y-yes?' Crinix B-Theta said.

'Do we have what you're looking for?'

They didn't. They really didn't, and Crinix B-Theta's terror suddenly returned. The thought of what UNIT might do if it found an Assessor watching its families. The thought of what the *Doctor* might do.

'I'm sorry,' Crinix B-Theta whispered, and fled.

'How did you know to stop me opening the door?' Fiona asked, when she was sure the thing was gone. 'That it wasn't Ali— that it wasn't Daddy?'

'You told me it was going to be all right,' Kate said simply. The two of them were sitting on the floor, Kate nestled between Fiona's legs the way she used to when she was small. Fiona hadn't let go of the gun yet. She wasn't sure she could.

'And?'

'I didn't believe you,' Kate said. 'I don't believe you. I want to . . . but I know you've been lying to me. About Daddy coming back.'

'I know,' Fiona said, and scrubbed tears from her cheek with the back of her hand. 'And I'm sorry, Kate.'

'You shouldn't lie,' Kate said. 'But now . . . now I know that you miss Daddy too.'

'Of *course* I miss him,' Fiona said. 'I miss him every day. And he wishes he was here too. I know he does. But –'

'Monsters,' Kate said solemnly.

'Right,' Fiona said. 'But we will see him. I promise. Just not right now. Right now, we need to figure out how to be on our own.'

Kate sniffed back tears, and then snuggled into the crook of Fiona's arm.

'I think you're doing OK so far.'

THE MYRIAPOD
MUTINY

EMMA NORRY

*I*n the beginning was darkness. Darkness and warmth. And that was all they needed – it was how their lives began. For millennia two underground species lived together side by side, each presided over by a master. Similar enough to co-exist, yet different enough to be wary of one another: allies more than friends. The slow and stoic we shall call the Under-trotters, the others, quick and quarrelsome, are known as the Side-steppers.

When the Great Freeze descended, they buried themselves deeper still and made a pact – to ensure, above all else, their mutual survival. Come what may. Yet neither foresaw the Great Collision which obliterated not only their planet, but their plans for survival too . . .

The Great Collision, 300 million years ago, catapulted huge rocks into the galaxy. What had once been their home was now ripped into

*pieces, tumbling through space and travelling immeasurable distances.
A few fragments rained down on to a planet rich in oxygen, burying
themselves deep in the ground. Over millions of years, traces of mineral,
silicate and crystals leaked into the soil, igniting growth in the unlikeliest
of places . . .*

'Year Seven!' Mr Cestin yelled, holding his hands up in that
familiar teacher gesture that means 'put a sock in it', as
twenty Year Sevens clambered noisily off the coach outside
the Natural History Museum. After almost three hours
cooped up, everyone was way too excited to be quiet.

Teachers handed out neon wristbands while children
leaned against the wall, waiting. 'This place has a massive
dinosaur,' Izzy said, popping gum and making herself the
centre of attention, as usual. 'My aunt lives round here. We
came loads when I was little.'

'Right!' Mr Cestin blew the sports whistle dangling
round his neck. 'Now. The plan for today is –'

Ryan Sinclair slipped an earphone in and zoned out.
He'd fallen asleep on the coach the minute it had set off, and
figured blasting a bit of Jay-Z might wake him up.

The class lined up to queue outside the museum
entrance. Ryan leaned against the ornate columns and watched
Ola and Tibo, his two best friends, punch each other in a

dead-arm contest. Ryan dodged out of their way – and caught the eye of Yasmin Khan, standing further ahead in the queue. Ryan and Yaz had been in the same class at Redlands Primary: Rosa Parks class. But since they'd arrived at secondary school, they'd barely crossed paths.

He had great memories of them hanging out in years Four and Five. They'd never fallen out exactly, but in many ways they were opposites. Yaz was in all the top sets and Ryan . . . well, school wasn't his favourite place.

'Turn that racket off, Ryan,' Ms Kadel barked. 'We're here to learn!'

Great. Ryan sighed and removed his earphone. Ms Kadel always gave him a hard time. Claimed he was skiving off when actually he just found it tricky to remember his way around such a big school. Ryan had tried to explain that his dyspraxia made a few things challenging – he often lost stuff, had almost unreadable handwriting and found it hard to concentrate, but she always thought the worst of him.

Mr Cestin blew his whistle again. 'Everyone with surnames A–M come with me, and N–Z are with Ms Kadel. Let's go!'

Twenty children scrambled into the right groups. Ryan said 'laters' to Ola and Tibo and hung back, watching the

A–M group follow Mr Cestin through the main doors. When Ryan's group eventually filtered through the entrance, they only walked a few steps before stopping again.

Ryan stared in awe at the skeleton of a gigantic dinosaur that occupied the entrance hall. *Incredible!* This place was like being inside a cathedral. Sunlight streamed in through the high windows and shafts of light highlighted the stained glass and mosaic floor.

'This is Hintze Hall,' Ms Kadel said.

Ryan glanced around, trying to get his bearings. Hintze Hall was a large open space with arches on either side.

'Those are the wonder bays,' Ms Kadel announced, pointing to them. 'Take a moment to appreciate the wooden monkeys and leaves carved into the walls. See the amazing ceiling which depicts the diverse plants from around the world.'

Ryan yawned. He was keen to see the cool stuff – not just the ceiling! Each wonder bay beneath the arch had a sign which gave information about the exhibit it housed. Behind the dinosaur skeleton was a big staircase with smaller staircases leading off either side, to another level above them. At the top of the stairs was a gigantic white statue of a man (obviously important, though Ryan didn't recognise him) sitting in a chair at the top.

'The museum is divided up into zones,' Ms Kadel said. 'We'll be going through to the green zone while the other group examine the blue zone and then we'll swap over.' She ushered them around one side of the hall, as Mr Cestin's group passed them. 'That's Charles Darwin, sitting at the top of the steps.'

Izzy took selfies in front of a giraffe. 'Oh my god!' She nudged her friends, screeching like a hyena. 'Look, it's got a neck almost as skinny as Yaz!'

Frowning, Yaz turned away from the exhibit, and bumped right into Ryan just as he'd stepped back to get a better look at the giraffe.

'Watch it!' she said, rubbing her elbow.

Ryan protested. 'It weren't me not looking where I was going!'

'Nice to see you too,' Yaz muttered, edging past him and keeping her distance from Izzy.

Catching up to the rest of his group, Ryan just caught the end of Ms Kadel's speech. '– after volcanoes and earthquakes, we'll have lunch in the cafe at one p.m. Keep your school jumpers on, please, even though it's warm. Next stop – creepy-crawlies, through here!'

Because of his dyspraxia, Ryan was sometimes unsteady on his feet, so while his group surged forward through yet more doors, he fell back, preferring space around him.

In the creepy-crawly room, everyone *oooh*ed and *ahh*ed at the spiders and insects pinned in the display cabinets. Some boys started running around the large model of a termite mound.

Ms Kadel droned on. 'The museum has over thirty million specimens of arthropods, including but not limited to: crabs, spiders, bees . . .'

Aaron, the class joker, pointed to a tarantula in a glass box. 'I heard that when you're asleep, you eat about eight spiders without even knowing it!'

A chorus of voices all said, 'Eww.'

Ryan winced. He wasn't scared of spiders, but still wouldn't want to wake up chewing on a furry, spindly leg, that was for sure.

Ms Kadel read aloud from an information panel. 'Spider silk is stronger than bone and can stretch up to three times its normal length.'

Ryan yawned again; Ms Kadel had a real talent for making even interesting things sound boring.

'Be careful!' Ms Kadel warned, after Ryan bumped into a display. It wasn't his fault that the kids were all standing so close together.

'Miss, I need the toilet.' Ryan knew he shouldn't have had that Fanta on the coach.

'Can't you wait?'

Embarrassed, Ryan shook his head.

Ms Kadel sighed. 'The toilets are next to the main door we just came through. You can't miss them. And don't be long!'

Ryan found the toilets easily enough, but when he came out he couldn't remember which direction he'd come from. And all the wonder bay arches looked the same! He glanced around but couldn't see anyone he recognised. Panic fluttering in his chest, he dodged a busy group of tourists and found a map of the museum on the back wall. He stared at the different-coloured zones, but still couldn't work out how to get back to the green zone.

He wondered who he should ask, but the hall had emptied out now and there was no one close by.

A bright glint caught his attention and he glanced down. On the floor in front of him was a long black-and-silver object, a bit like a slim torch. Ryan picked it up. Who'd dropped this? Turning it over, he noticed tiny buttons on the side and pressed a few to see if they did anything. *Nothing.* He shook it. Still nothing. *Maybe it needs new batteries.* He stuffed it into his pocket, thinking he could hand it in to lost property later on.

He peered again at the map. He could just explore on his own for a bit. There was loads of weird stuff here and there was no way their group would have time to look at half of it. The mineral room and vault sounded cool, and according to the map they would be easy to find too – literally right above him. As long as he was in the cafe by 1 p.m., what was the problem? He doubted Ms Kadel would miss him.

Confident in his decision, Ryan bounded up the massive staircase and nodded to the giant Darwin statue, before turning right and heading up the smaller staircase.

He stopped to draw breath in front of a glass cabinet housing a gorilla called Guy. 'All right, big fella?' Ryan smirked.

He pressed his lips right up against the glass and blew his cheeks out.

On their planet the myriapods had been giants, as the oxygen levels were significantly greater. Here, though, they had evolved to a fraction of their original magnificent size. But, over time, they adapted to their tiny stature, and gained knowledge, gathered information, discovered what they were capable of. Now miniscule, they closely resembled the millipedes and centipedes who already inhabited this Earth. Both Under-trotters and Side-steppers became adept at remaining unharmed because they were mainly unseen. They learned how to move quickly and relished being able to operate in this new world without detection or interference. And there

*was food aplenty. The armies vowed to bide their time until the elders —
their masters — reawakened from their suspended animation and called
them. There was plenty here for the taking.*

On his way to the mineral room, Ryan had stopped along the
corridor to admire a wall full of colourful butterflies and
beetles pinned up in a big display.

'Ryan!'

He jerked round to see who'd called his name.

It was Yaz. She walked towards him, cheeks red, biting
her fingernails. 'I've lost my group!'

Ryan smiled, relieved to see a familiar face. 'Me too.'

Yaz's hair, usually in neat long plaits, had frizzed out at
the sides and her shirt was untucked. 'Think we'll get in
trouble?'

'I'm not really in a rush to get back.' He shrugged.

'I only went to fill up my water bottle . . .' She trailed off
and moved out of the way of a group of squealing primary-
school children who came rushing past.

Ryan gave Yaz what he hoped was a reassuring grin. 'We
can hang out together.'

Yaz bit her lip. 'I should find my group . . .' She trailed
off again, twisting her hands.

'Isn't it better to stay away from Izzy, if you can?'

Yaz sighed and stared at the floor.

'What's her problem, anyway?' Ryan asked, gently. He knew she'd been badmouthing Yaz for a while; everyone knew.

'She hates not being the best at everything.'

'Heard you knocked her off the maths leaderboard. Nice one.'

Yaz gave a little smile. 'Sure did.' She scuffed her shoe back and forth on the tiled floor.

'There's amazing stuff here. They've got real *meteorites* in the mineral room. And behind that there's like a vault thing with crystals, gems and gold. Want to have a look?'

Yaz's smile was wide. 'Where's this meteorite, then?'

But they were constantly on the guard against attack.

But eventually, the quick and quarrelsome grew dissatisfied and, without leadership from their masters, who were still in stasis, dissent set in. Instead of working together, the quick noticed how the slow and stoic turned away from flesh and meat. The slow had characteristics that the quick did not: more legs and a hard, protective outer shell. They avoided trouble and would curl up in an instant, always remaining calm and peaceful. The quarrelsome, always left to defend, became resentful and felt inferior . . . where was their armour? They had none. Even though they had poison at their disposal, they always felt threatened, vulnerable. They relied on their wits and caught their prey without being detected. Their mouths were hidden beneath their heads. But they were constantly on guard against attack . . .

When they reached the mineral room, at the end of the corridor, Yaz followed Ryan in. Apart from a small group of American tourists, the place was empty.

'This is just old stones – boring!' Yaz said, grinning mischievously. The room was vast, with rows and rows of glass-topped wooden cabinets lining the floor, and more display cabinets on the walls.

'It's not boring.' Ryan shook his head. 'There's real gold nuggets over here!'

They peered into cabincts filled with rocks of different shapes and sizes. A security guard sat at the back, snoring lightly. They looked at each other and burst into giggles.

When they'd calmed down, Yaz sighed. 'Can't believe we haven't spoken since leaving Redlands.'

Ryan scratched the back of his neck. 'I know, it's mad, innit?' He didn't know what else to say; they'd been good friends back in the day. 'Secondary school's well harder.'

'Yeah.' Yaz nodded. 'I kind of miss those days.'

'Come on, bet the vault has even better stuff.' Ryan pointed to the entrance at the back of the room. As they walked through, Yaz looked up at the heavy metal shutter above the entrance. 'Wouldn't want to get trapped in here – it's like something out of *Mission Impossible*!'

'Look at this!' Ryan beckoned Yaz over to a cabinet and pressed his nose right up against the glass.

'What's that?' she asked.

Ryan started reading the text displayed next to the exhibit: 'This is a Martian meteorite called Nakhla.' He gazed at it in wonder. 'From *Mars*. Man, I love space. How crazy is that . . . this rock is from another planet!'

Yaz rolled her eyes. 'Calm down, Doctor Spock!' She shook her head. '*Star Wars* isn't really my thing.'

Ryan grinned. '*Star Trek* is sci-fi, *Star Wars* is more like fantasy, really.'

'If you say so. Now look, over there is the world's biggest emerald. *That's* what I call impressive.'

'Remember that space project we did in Year Four?' asked Ryan, giving Yaz a friendly shove.

'Yeah!' Yaz laughed. 'A solar system made from fruit, and you ate Jupiter!' She pushed Ryan back, nudging him sideways.

Caught off guard, Ryan stumbled forward and banged his hip hard into the cabinet. Suddenly, his pocket vibrated and a series of bleeps and beeps started.

Ryan patted his pocket, bringing out the mini torch he'd found earlier. It felt warm. As it lit up in his hand, he dropped it, right on to the cabinet. The meteorite inside – balancing on a pedestal – rocked back and forth. Ryan flinched, watching the rock wobble, and then gulped as the meteorite fell against its case. A sharp edge banged into the glass, chipping it.

Yaz gasped. 'What have you done?!'

'I'm out of here!' Ryan moved to leave, but Yaz grabbed his arm and pulled him forward.

'Look.' She peered at where the rock had struck the glass. 'It's cracked the glass and . . . that crack is getting bigger!'

Ryan leaned in closer. A high-pitched whine hissed out of the crack, as if someone was letting air out slowly from a balloon. Zigzags sprinted along the glass, like the ice on a pond breaking up.

Ryan couldn't take his eyes off the splintering glass, or the stone, which was now jerking and bouncing, as if it was somehow alive.

'Yaz, can you hear that noise coming from the cabinet?'

'No.' Yaz frowned. 'Can't hear anything. Should we find someone?'

They both stared as the meteorite suddenly shook violently and then split into five separate pieces. Ryan could have sworn that he saw something moving on one of the inner faces.

'Uh-oh.' Ryan muttered. 'This can't be good. Let's get out of here!'

Back in the mineral room, the security guard was nowhere to be seen. The place was empty. Weird for a museum, especially in the middle of London.

As they left and found themselves back in the corridor, a shiver passed across Ryan's shoulders. He wiggled his finger in his ear, trying to get rid of the whine he'd started hearing when the glass case cracked open.

They couldn't see a single person. *Where was everyone?*

At the top of the stairs, Ryan stopped next to Darwin. 'You still can't hear that whining noise?' he asked, straining.

Yaz was on the stairs below him. 'Maybe it's like them dog whistles that only you can hear?'

Ryan heard other noises now too. Except these were like scuttling and scurrying, and were coming from everywhere . . . above, below and all around. He tried to work out where this new noise was coming from.

Instead of wanting companions or allies, the quarrelsome wanted what they did not have: power. The masters of neither species had yet awoken from their suspended animation and the quick were impatient. The masters had promised them rewards. The quarrelsome soon asserted dominance over the slow and stoic. Their front legs were now sharp, pointed claws with which they could inject enzymes into their prey, rendering them helpless. They whispered to the slow how one day their time would come; how one day they would rule. They were sure the masters, when their time came, would agree.

'What. Are. *They?*' Ryan pointed at the smaller staircase opposite them.

Yaz stared and rubbed her eyes. 'Are they . . . worms?' she said, fear creeping into her voice.

Ryan stepped forward to peer at them. 'I dunno, but there's hundreds of them!'

Almost side by side now, Ryan and Yaz both stared at the clumps of writhing insects crawling over the staircases.

'Where did they come from?' Yaz asked, sounding panicked. 'Do you reckon they . . . bite?'

Even though he had no idea what it was, Ryan pulled the mini torch out of his pocket and waved it at the insects facing him. 'Don't take your eyes off the ones on your side!'

Suddenly the insects facing Ryan bunched up tight, about the size of a beach ball, and then shot out fast in various directions. Hundreds of tiny writhing forms dispersed across the staircases, burrowing into cracks and crevices until they'd disappeared completely.

Yaz and Ryan turned to one another, mouths open. 'Where did they go?'

'Did you see their legs!' Ryan exclaimed. Thinking about their hurried, scuttling movements made him feel itchy. They'd moved so fast he hadn't known where to look. He'd never seen that many insects in one place before.

'They definitely aren't worms . . . were they centipedes?' Yaz said.

'Or millipedes?' Ryan said. 'Don't they have their legs under their body?'

Yaz grimaced. 'What's the difference?'

'A great deal, actually,' came a voice. 'Ah, good-oh! You've found it!'

The pair whipped round to see a man, with some sort of recorder dangling from one hand, staring at Yaz and Ryan, holding out his other hand towards them. His eyes, set above a prominent nose, shone, making him look permanently surprised, and he had dark bushy eyebrows. His mop of straight black hair fell over his bright eyes, and the navy bow tie and brown checked trousers gave him a sort of odd professor look.

'I'd be in so much trouble with Glaxion 6 if that got into the wrong hands.' The man pocketed the recorder and wiggled his index finger. 'May I trouble you for my sonic?' When he smiled, he looked mischievous and excited at the same time.

It took a moment for Ryan to realise that the man meant the mini torch in his hand. He reluctantly handed it over.

'What is that?' Yaz asked. 'What does it do?'

The man shuffled closer, staring at them hard. 'A better question might be – what doesn't it do!' He chuckled, waving the long silver instrument. 'Ah, back where you belong.'

Yaz and Ryan gave each other a wary look. They were constantly reminded by adults never to talk to strangers . . . and this man was about as strange as you could get.

'This marvelous device is called a sonic screwdriver. It's very handy indeed. Does a billion and one things! An *actual* billion and one. As for those wriggly critters? They're myriapods – the many-legged beings. On Earth you'd easily mistake them for centipedes and millipedes, but *these* particular specimens are over 428 million years old and from a different planet altogether, actually. We call them the Side-steppers and Under-trotters.'

'You're not serious?' Ryan laughed, eyes wide. 'A different planet?'

'You mean, they're *alien*?' Yaz was open-mouthed. 'You're winding us up, right?'

The man held his screwdriver up to the light and twiddled the top of it.

'I'm very serious! These leggy beasts were bigger than the brown bear at one point in time, but when they landed on this planet they shrank. The untrained eye wouldn't be able to tell them apart from centipedes or millipedes, but the masters – the Adam and Eve of the species, if you like – lay dormant in fragments of asteroid for millions of years, constantly emitting a high-pitched whine . . . almost a rescue beacon. It was only because of the crack in the glass that their faithful soldiers could hear them, finally. They've been living underneath this museum since before it was built. Now, they're assembling from all over.'

Ryan wasn't sure what he was saying. He tried to catch Yaz's eye, but she couldn't stop staring at the old man.

'How come you know all this?'

'If you're joking, then it's a really weird joke,' Ryan said, thinking that they ought to leave this man alone.

The man frowned and tilted his head to one side, his eyes lively.

'This is no joke, I can assure you,' he said. 'It's my . . . job to ascertain what they want, why they're here – then check in about when they plan to leave. They've been waiting for their masters for a long time and might prove trickier to persuade to leave than I thought. I've some tips for you, if you'd like. Keep your hands in your pockets so they don't crawl up your sleeves. Tuck your trousers into your – *ahhh.*'

He glanced at Yaz and her school skirt, dismayed.

'Given your lack of proper attire, you, young lady, might wish to take extra care. They're speedy, and will bite any ankle within reach! Now that the masters have awoken, they're gathering all their troops, trying to mobilise. Soon you won't be able to move for them. I strongly suggest making your way promptly to the exit. The rest of the museum has already been evacuated – I may have had a little play with the smoke alarm.' He smiled slyly.

Yaz gave Ryan a doubtful glance. 'I didn't hear the smoke alarm.'

'The high-pitched signal from the vault blocked it. You two wouldn't have been able to hear it over that.' He turned to Ryan. 'That was the noise you mentioned.'

'Why could only I hear it?'

The man shrugged. 'Not sure, but maybe you've just been blessed with exceptional hearing?'

'Who *are* you?' Yaz asked, staring at him suspiciously.

The man smiled. 'I'm many things: a caretaker, a curator, a health-and-safety inspector and a doctor, to name but a few. You can call me Doctor, for now. You'd best leave – if these myriapods get too close, they'll suck out your brains before you know it.'

'Haha – very funny,' Ryan said.

But the old man wasn't smiling now. 'Where better than a damp, warm, pulsating human brain to lay eggs and ensure the survival of your species?' Staring at them, he blinked several times in a row. 'They want to see if they can get back to their original size and prominent position! And if that happens then we've all had it, I'm afraid.'

Ryan and Yaz didn't need to be told again; they hurtled down the stairs and stood panting in Hintze Hall. Ryan blinked and rubbed his eyes. For a moment it seemed that the monkeys and leaves engraved in the arches had come to life. But when he looked closer he realised the centipedes and millipedes – hundreds, maybe even thousands of them – were skittering along the floor, running up the walls. Scrabbling and scratching in every direction. The wonder bays and floor were alive, writhing and twisting.

'Stay away from the Side-steppers!' the man yelled after them. 'They're the dangerous ones!'

'They all look the same!' shouted Yaz, trying to dodge a thrashing pile as they clustered and swarmed over each other, knitting together. A low buzz pulsed through the air, the sound of a billion tiny legs tapping in unison.

Some had rolled themselves up into tiny balls and scattered across the floor, bouncing off each other. Others tried to crawl over the balled-up ones, enveloping them. A hideous smell of rotting leaves, damp bark and decaying carcasses filled the air.

Ryan pulled the front of his jumper over his nose. 'How can we get out?!' He turned to see the man scanning the area with his sonic screwdriver. 'The exit's totally blocked!'

The creatures with legs out to the side moved like tiny snakes, slithering from side to side, skilfully, and sneakily, disappearing into every available hole or gap.

'No time for chitchat – you two need to go!' The man examined the screwdriver, reading information scrolling up a panel that had appeared in the side.

'No chance that thing is a weapon as well as a screwdriver?' Ryan asked.

'Not quite – but it is what will save us – hopefully.'

'Look!' Yaz pointed to six feet ahead of them. 'They're everywhere! I'm going back up –' She grasped the bannister and then let go immediately. 'Eww!' She shook her hand.

Ryan gagged as a half-squashed centipede flew into the air. Then a shiny black millipede dropped from the ceiling on to Yaz's shirt collar. She tried to brush it off, but it wriggled along her jumper. Ryan shuddered as it disappeared into her ear, white legs wiggling furiously.

'What was that?' she said, spinning round and slapping at her neck manically.

'I think –' Ryan couldn't find the words.

Suddenly, Yaz's body stiffened completely. Her arms went rigid at her sides. Her eyes twitched, the pupils shuddering and turning milky.

'Yaz – you OK?'

Her eyes narrowed, her head tilted right back, and her mouth opened slowly. Another creature, fatter and longer than the one which had slipped into her ear, emerged from between her lips. Its legs waggled furiously.

Ryan shivered, the hairs on the back of his neck all raised. He was terrified. 'Doctor, help her! What's it *doing*?'

The Doctor leaped across the staircase and peered at Yaz's lips. 'Ah . . . hmm. Not good at all, I'm afraid!'

Ryan flinched as half of the creature in Yaz's ear dangled out, like a telephone cord. 'Is she all right?'

The Doctor scanned her lips and ears and rotated his screwdriver. 'The myriapods will use her in some rudimentary way – they may need a vessel, a voice. There appears to be no threat to life. Not as far as I can tell. Yet.'

The slow and stoic want to rise up, to end their persecution. They want to be free: to eat what they want, to live in peace. They want to extend and enrich this Earth. They have come to see it as home – the breathing bark and succulent soil. They can help grow the forests and reinvigorate ecosystems. They have witnessed the destruction and eradication of too many species. They understand exactly what this Earth needs and are keen to help, unlike their quarrelsome counterparts who only seek to dominate.

Yaz's mouth opened wider and a nasal rasp came out, sounding like a human with a very bad cold, punctuated by crisp clicks and clacks.

'I use this carbon-based life form in order to communicate in a way you will comprehend.'

Yaz's eyes remained cloudy and blank.

Ryan was shaking. *What is happening?* He found it impossible to believe he was listening to an alien insect that had taken over Yaz's body. Was Yaz still in there? Was she all right?

'We are released. Now we can take our rightful place and release all who have waited so patiently.'

'All of whom?' The Doctor demanded, now standing next to Ryan.

'All of us buried in the earth. In the rocks, the fossils, under the oceans.'

The Doctor held up his screwdriver, scanning the insect as he questioned it. 'What do you want?'

Yaz lurched forward and then thrust her body back – her head shook so fast that it looked like it might fall right off. The slithery creature which had been hanging from her lips vanished into her other ear and a loud, high-pitched screeching filled the air. Darting in and out of Yaz's nose and in-between her lips, the Side-stepper and the Under-trotter tangled together, wrestling strenuously.

'Stop this at once!' The Doctor frantically searched his pockets.

'What are you looking for?' Ryan asked.

'I need something long and strong, like string or wire . . .' He patted himself down. 'Haven't got time to get to the TARDIS . . .' he muttered.

Ryan stuck his hand in his pocket and brought out his headphones. He held them up. 'These do?'

'Perfect! Most useful.' The Doctor plugged them into his screwdriver and stepped in front of Yaz. He wrapped the cable around the Side-stepper, which stopped its thrashing.

'Now. Listen – you had your turn. Let the other speak . . .'

The Under-trotter rose and waggled its white legs, hundreds of them. It sounded softer and slower – more a whispering *mulch-slush*, like being dragged through wet mud, than the crisp, clear *clickety-clack* of the Side-stepper.

Ryan leaned in close to the Doctor and whispered. 'How's it talking?'

'They're using their legs as a sort of antenna to connect with the frontal lobes and explore both the Broca and Wernicke areas,' he replied. 'Simply put, it's tickling her brain to make her talk.'

'We seek only sanctuary. Solace. We come to serve. But the Side-steppers have taken over and – *mulch-slush*!'

The Under-trotter twisted, rolled up and retreated into Yaz's nose.

'Cowards!' thundered the Doctor. 'Leave her alone – if you want to convey your message, you do so through me.'

Violet light emanated from the screwdriver.

'State your purpose on this planet and what you want. We can come to an arrangement, I'm sure.'

A confused chorus of beeps and whirs came from the screwdriver buttons as he pressed them.

Click-clack-click. Yaz tilted her head to one side. The Side-stepper poked out of her ear, its other end thrashing out of her nose. Its antennae waved around, and its legs flailed wildly. Both myriapods then disentangled themselves and crawled out of Yaz, scuttling across the floor to the Doctor.

Yaz stood stock-still, her eyes closed.

Ryan cringed as the insects crawled into the Doctor's ear. The Doctor chuckled as if being tickled and then inserted his sonic screwdriver into his other ear.

Running over to Yaz, Ryan put his hand on her shoulder. She felt cold to the touch. He tried kicking out at the swarm that had gathered around his ankles. They seemed to be chasing each other and fighting, thrashing, darting and scattering back and forth and then retreating.

'We demand control,' said the *click-clack* voice.

'Control of what?' asked Ryan, not sure if he was addressing the insects or the Doctor.

'Everything!' exclaimed the Side-stepper.

The Doctor grinned and grimaced, grappling to retain control over his own speech. He spoke with a lot of effort, his voice unusually loud and slow.

'Listen. That's not how things work. And especially not here, my friends. The name of the game, if you want a long and happy life on this spinning rock, is . . . compromise.'

The Side-stepper withdrew and a series of ticks and clicks could be heard.

'What's happening?' Ryan looked confused.

'They're processing and decoding,' the Doctor replied. 'They need time to translate and respond; they'll leave me alone while they do that.'

'How can I help her?' Ryan looked desperately at his friend, who still wasn't moving. His voice shook. 'Will she be OK?'

The Doctor nodded. 'She's in a temporary state of paralysis. The Side-steppers, the ones most like centipedes, paralyse their prey with venom, so it'll wear off in five minutes. I already took an antidote. Based on the research I've gathered, the masters of these creatures — their oldest ancestors — were hibernating, buried in the oldest meteorite on Earth. The one in the vault. When you bumped this little chap,' he said, gesturing at his screwdriver, 'you set off a cosmic alarm clock. It didn't take these old bedfellows long to remember their differences and summon their myriapod armies.'

'We do not compromise,' came their reply.

The Doctor sighed. 'Assimilate or we'll need to consider an alternative.'

More whirring and humming and then a deathly, spiky silence.

'Look,' the Doctor said impatiently. 'From the readings I've established, the armoured ones are just more naturally suited to this environment. The Under-trotters eat decomposing organic matter. This adds to decomposition and nutrients being recycled. This planet needs them; they *help*. A mutually beneficial arrangement, otherwise known as symbiosis. Ideal really. You *could* fit in quite happily here too, but not if you insist on control and dominance.'

'We do not assimilate.'

Ryan wasn't sure, but he thought the Side-stepper sounded almost sulky.

'Right. Well . . .' The Doctor thought for a while. 'Looks like our peace talks have come to an impasse, then.' He twirled the screwdriver and the Under-trotter dropped out of his mouth, while the Side-stepper twisted and hissed out of his ear. They scurried away, clicking and whistling.

Yaz gave a huge gasp. Ryan spun to look at her, worried.

'You feeling OK?'

She blinked and rubbed at her eyes. 'Um, I *think* so,' she said, uncertainly. 'What just happened? Feels like I need to blow my nose.'

'Good to see you're still with us,' the Doctor said. 'Now, Yasmin is it? Sorry to press you, but with them tickling your frontal cortex, you'll have absorbed some of their history . . .'

Ryan stared at the Doctor, worry crossing his features. The Doctor waved his hands around. 'Oh, me? Don't you worry about me. My brain is so ancient and layered they wouldn't have stood a chance getting me to absorb anything. It's the young growing brains they prefer. So, Yaz, any ways we can stop a war come to mind? Anything you might have seen when they were burrowing away in there?'

'Me?' Yaz blinked in surprise. 'Erm, well . . . I did get flashes of some strange images . . . If they can't get along living together then maybe one lot could go somewhere else? There must be a place that'll suit them. What do they like?'

'Meat, heat, dense tropical – aha!' The Doctor jumped in the air. 'Side-steppers!' As he spoke, he waved his screwdriver low on the ground and a beam of green light shone out, accompanied by alternating *click-clacks* and the mulchy-slushy sound that the Under-trotters had made.

'Listen up, Side-steppers, this is the deal! I happen to know the perfect habitat. It's just become vacant and needs clearing up. Rotting flesh everywhere, you'd be doing the universe a favour.'

Skittering, scrambling, whirring and clacking while both species conferred. Some hissing and spitting.

Yaz yelled, 'The Doctor's offering you a good deal! This way everyone wins, right? He's a man of his word.'

The Doctor gave a little bow in Yaz's direction. 'I am indeed a man of my word. She's correct in her assessment. Now, Under-trotters, you may remain here. Vacate this museum, and go underground, find your bark and slabs and dig in. Side-steppers, follow me.'

Thousands of myriapods *click-clack*ed and poured out from every crevice in the hall.

A long trail of Side-steppers, thousands piled on top of one another, slid along behind the Doctor as he walked across the foyer. His recorder was now pressed to his lips as he ambled along, playing a tune that could barely be heard over the din of clicks and clacks. They followed him to a tall rectangular blue box that stood just to the right of the gift shop.

'What's that?' Yaz pointed to the box.

'It's one of them old-fashioned phone boxes, you know, except they're usually red,' Ryan replied.

They watched the Doctor usher the centipedes inside. He closed the door and came back towards Ryan and Yaz . . .

So the Under-trotters found their home on Earth, and the Side-steppers left to cross the stars, in search of somewhere new. As is the way with their species, they left no trace that they had been on Earth – not even a memory . . .

People filed back into the museum. The staircase was clear now – no centipedes or millipedes anywhere to be seen.

As Yaz and Ryan moved aside to let people get back up the stairs, Ms Kadel, her face red and forehead sweaty as she stormed over, glared at them.

'Ryan Sinclair and Yasmin Khan!'

Mr Cestin appeared behind her, and the rest of the kids soon surrounded them.

'You two are in for it now!' crowed Izzy.

'That's enough, Izzy,' Mr Cestin said. 'Where have you two been?'

'And what have you been doing?' barked Ms Kadel.

Ryan and Yaz stared blankly at each other. What *had* they been doing? The last thing either of them remembered was getting lost and looking at some meteorite together.

'Skiving!' Ms Kadel narrowed her eyes. 'I knew it! The one activity Ryan excels at! Young man, we're here to learn and if you can't do that –'

'Actually, miss . . .' Ryan took a deep breath and stared at her directly. Although his head felt a bit fuzzy, he was clear and confident when he spoke. 'This museum is sick; thanks for bringing us. After I got lost, I did some investigating.'

'We both did.' Yaz smiled at Mr Cestin, ignoring Ms Kadel. 'Ryan found out some very interesting stuff.'

Ryan felt a fluttering in his chest, but the good kind this time, and he started to speak again, not exactly sure what would come out.

'Did you know that arthropod means "jointed body"? And millipedes – they're well ancient. They evolved in the Precambrian oceans, like over four hundred million years ago. The millipede was the earliest land animal, and centipedes and millipedes – well, they don't actually have a hundred or a thousand legs.'

Ms Kadel gawped at Ryan.

'Glad to see you used your time wisely.' Mr Cestin smiled. 'Good for you, Ryan.'

Ms Kadel cleared her throat. 'Well yes, anyway. Everyone to the cafe! Follow me, please.'

Soon the air was filled with the noise of everyone talking loudly about what they wanted to eat, what they'd seen, what they were going to do later. Ryan found the chatter strangely comforting.

As Yaz went past to join her group again, she leaned towards Ryan. 'Nice one,' she said, grinning. 'Catch you later.'

Ryan smiled back at her. He couldn't quite remember exactly what they'd been doing, but he knew he'd enjoyed himself. He understood that once they were back at school, she'd still hang out with her friends, and he'd be with his. But he had the strangest feeling that one day they'd hang out together again. He was sure of it.

THE LAST OF
THE DALS

TEMI OH

There are many legends involving Davros, Skaro and the Daleks. Some are completely true. And some are simply myths, stories and cautionary tales, told to keep the citizens of the universe entertained – and afraid. This story is one of those myths. The Dals are a whispered legend. Little is known about them, and nothing for certain. The idea that they can tell the future, that they bear any relation to Kaleds and Thals . . . such questions can never be answered, and certainly not by two young adventurers on a quest to discover the future.

But though the story that follows is shrouded in half-lies and legend, its warning is very real indeed . . .

Davros still jolts awake sometimes to discover that his sleep-dazed brain has conjured hand-mines from the bedroom floor. The rug sinks, becomes viscous and swampy. Bumps jut from its surface, then peel themselves free as fingers. His blood turns to ice. He's surrounded. Any sudden motion will doom him. A hot clay palm will slap his ankle, clutch it in a death grip, and before he knows it, he'll be pulled down into oblivion.

The dream always ends at the very worst moment – when his heart is completely frozen in terror. He never gets to relive the hour of his unexpected salvation, when the man in the box appeared. The man who had trembled at the sound of his name. Though Davros always awakes thinking of him.

In fact, such is the vividness of the dream, that sometimes Davros isn't all that sure that he's even woken up . . .

The night of his father's funeral, he has the dream again. Upon waking, he does what he always does: leans over the side of the bed – too afraid to risk the floor – and reaches for a locked box, opening it with the key he keeps round his neck. Inside is the screwdriver. At least, that's what the man had called it, before he gave it to Davros.

Davros has his suspicions, but it's been almost a decade now since his sister Yarvell dared him to leave the relative safety of their domed city and venture into that no man's land where the eternal war between the Thals and the Kaleds rages. Since then, the screwdriver has become something of a talisman to him. The only way to prove it really happened.

It's an interesting device, like nothing he's ever seen before. Over the years he's examined and considered every part of it. The leather grip, the sonic generator coil, the power cell, and the emitter crystal at the top. It's the crystal that puzzles him more than anything. It's a kind of alien green that appears to change with the light outside: juniper to sea foam. It's made from some undiscovered element, which his research suggests is older than anything in the known universe. Davros has hesitantly hypothesised that the screwdriver could be some relic from the future, and, in some wild moments, he suspects that the man who saved him could have been as well. A wizard or a time traveller.

A knock at the door. 'Davros?' It's his mother, Lady Calcula. Davros scrambles to put the screwdriver away before she pushes the door open.

'Night terrors?' she asks. She looks as if she hasn't slept much either, judging by the puce shadows under her eyes.

'One,' he says.

'I wonder if I'll ever sleep soundly again,' she says, more to herself than to him.

It's been only a fortnight since Davros' father, Colonel Nasgard, was killed. The colonel was a senior officer in the Kaled Military Elite and his death has rattled Davros. 'I keep thinking,' he says now, letting his eyes drift to the window where their moonlit reflections float like phantoms, 'it could have been any of us.'

His mother winces. 'Don't talk like that.'

'But,' Davros says, sitting further up in bed, 'that's the thing about war.' He can't stop thinking about the bomb that killed his father and aunt. The suddenness and unexpectedness of it reminds him how uncertain his own future is. Davros dreams of being great, and yet, as a child of an interminable war, he understands how swiftly all his ambitions could come to nothing.

The initial cause of the thousand-year war is lost to history, but, still, the Kaleds and the Thals have fought for generations. As a result of their conflict, the planet is ravaged by radiation and most of its inhabitants now live in domed cities. From the window of his bedroom, Davros sometimes thinks he can make out the crescent dome of the Thal city in the distance. Whenever he thinks of the Thals, his gut twists with loathing. He imagines them prowling their sprawling streets, thirsty for Kaled blood.

'Don't trouble yourself,' his mother says now, 'about things that always have been and always will be.'

'But is that true? Will it always be?'

His mother wants him to join the Military Youth, but the thought of it somehow bores and terrifies him in equal measure. He imagines being swallowed up, a cog or a spur in the ancient machine. He doesn't want to be part of the war. He wants to end it, once and for all.

Davros is hiding in the university's petrified garden the afternoon the boy approaches to ask if he'd like to know his future.

Davros came to the university to ask a professor about the screwdriver. Professor Cypher, who specialises in rare Skarosian metals. It was a mistake, he realises now. He had been delighted to enter the university's expansive campus, to roam the halls and linger by the classrooms, lecture theatres and labs. To allow himself the fleeting daydream of a life in the ranks of the scientific elite, instead of the military.

Professor Cypher gave him a relatively warm welcome, but as soon as Davros produced the screwdriver the expression on the man's face darkened. Even now, Davros is not sure what he glimpsed in the professor's eyes. Rage? Confusion? Terror?

'Where did you get this?' he asked, some tension creeping into his voice as he grabbed the screwdriver in a way that made Davros worry he would never give it back.

'None of your business,' Davros snapped, suddenly defensive. He lunged forward, snatched the device back, and made a beeline for the door. Before he could reach it, though, the professor sounded the alarm and guards materialised in the corridors. It was all Davros could do to scrabble out of the open window, falling to his knees as he landed, the siren wailing behind him.

Davros dashed through the garden, bare branches catching at his clothes as he ran. At the sound of boots coming up a perpendicular footpath, he took cover behind a gnarled tree.

Now Davros squeezes his eyes closed as he listens to the squadron move further away. He lets himself exhale in relief but is startled when he looks around to spot two purple eyes blinking in the shadows. At first, he expects to find another armoured guard, but instead he is face to face with a boy who looks a little younger than him: fifteen or sixteen. He tells Davros that his name is Elwyn.

They're forced to fall silent then, as the heavy boots of another squadron crunch the ground. Davros pushes himself up against the hard bark of the tree, hoping to vanish in the shadows.

'Who are you?' he whispers.

'Prescient,' the boy says. 'Well, that's *what* I am. And only sometimes. Would you believe me if I told you that I've been dreaming for years of this moment? Of finding you here?'

'You'd be surprised at the things I'd believe,' Davros says. He's thinking about the screwdriver in his pocket, the man who could have been from the future.

Elwyn smiles as if he already understands and says, 'I'm one of the last descendants of the Dals.'

'Impossible,' Davros whispers again. Everything he'd ever heard about the Dals was shrouded in myth and folk tale. For years, Davros had believed that they had been an ancient indigenous people, who, it was rumoured, possessed the ability to see the future. Now he's not sure what's true.

Although most of the books of Dal myths were confiscated and burned, a copy of the *Book of Predictions* has been preserved in Davros' family. Davros used it to teach himself some of the language supposed to have been spoken by them.

Davros decides to test this boy with one of the few phrases that he remembers. '*How can it be true?*'

'*A few survived,*' Elwyn says, but then translates it into Kaled when he sees that Davros doesn't understand. 'A handful, maybe. My great-great-great-grandmother was one of them. Most of us live in hiding, in small communities on the edge of the dome.'

In myths and legends, the Dals have purple eyes and silver hair. Elwyn has blond hair, though, grown long and tied at the top of his head. He says, 'I've been haunted for a while by a vision. A notion. That a boy with a screwdriver is going to end the war.'

The words hit Davros like a lightning bolt to the sternum.

'M-me?' he asks, his voice shallow.

'I don't know.' Elwyn glances down at the pocket where Davros hid the screwdriver.

At any other time, Davros might have laughed him off. But he's been thinking more and more about the uncertain future that lies ahead of him. Thinking about the time traveller he encountered as a child. 'I want to know,' he says shakily. 'I want to know about the future.'

By now, the guards seem to have returned to the university, satisfied that Davros is no longer on the premises. The siren stops ringing, leaving a tinnitus trill in Davros' ears.

Elwyn smiles, then he explains that the last true Dal has lived for hundreds of years in the ruins of their capital city. He claims that many people he knows have made pilgrimages to see her. He tells Davros that if she lays her hands on you, you may see a vision of your own future.

The thought of this grips Davros immediately. He would love nothing more than to glimpse his future, to see what kind of a man he will become. In his daydreams there's a larger-than-life statue of him oxidising in their city's square, peace reigns and he is celebrated as the man who finally won the war. Maybe he does this as a great military general; maybe he becomes the man his father never had the chance to be. Perhaps, if he follows Elwyn, he will discover how it happens.

'I want to do it,' Davros says.

Elwyn explains that if he is ready to go on the pilgrimage they will need to meet at a certain spot, outside the city's protective dome, in eleven days.

Davros hesitates.

'You've been outside the dome before, right?' Elwyn asks.

'Right,' Davros says a little distantly. 'But the last time . . .' The last time, he'd almost been killed by hand-mines.

Sensing his hesitation, Elwyn says, 'Look, if you're not ready for it, I –'

'Of course I'm ready,' Davros protests. Elwyn looks doubtful. Many Kaleds, the lucky ones, never leave the protective dome of their city.

'It's not an easy journey,' Elwyn says. To get to the Dal city, he explains, they will have to cross the Lake of Mutations, then attempt a perilous climb up the Drammakins mountains. And it's not a simple thing, Elwyn warns, to see one's future. Everybody who does is changed forever.

But there is nothing he can say that will dissuade Davros now. A chance to uncover some of the mystery of the Dals. He reaches out to shake the boy's hand. 'I want to go,' Davros says, 'I'm ready.'

They meet at sunrise, on the edge of the city. Davros had slept little the night before. Had waited until the house was quiet to grab his bag – hastily packed with a couple of changes of clothes, tinned food from the family bunker and, of course, his screwdriver.

Davros gives a false name to the distracted attendant at the city gates. Though he knows it won't make much of a difference: Kaleds pay more attention to people trying to get into the city than anyone who wants to leave. 'At your own peril,' the attendant says.

'They say that to everyone,' Elwyn whispers. He's wearing his hood low over his forehead to hide the purple shade of his eyes from the guard.

The sky looks different on the other side of the Kaleds' opalescent dome. Radioactive. Weak sunlight shimmers through gas clouds. Particles of dust glitter in the air. It smells of sulphur, smoke and blood.

'It's the iron,' Elwyn says, kicking the soil with the toe of his well-worn sandal. It's a ferric-red clay.

Most of the planet has been scarred and petrified after centuries of war. To try to live for any length of time outside the protective dome of the city is to expose your body to an onslaught of radiation, and the many dangers that lurk in the lakes and the mountains.

'The potassium iodide I brought should help us for a little while,' Elwyn says.

'Have you made this journey before?' Davros asks.

'Only once,' he admits, 'with my father.'

'And what happened?'

'He died.'

The sun is almost setting when they arrive at the Lake of Mutations. They've walked the whole day through long-abandoned hamlets, towns and villages.

The lake looks vast and terrible in the moonlight. Notjust because of the dark water – which is reported to cause chemical burns on contact – but because Davros knows that creatures are lurking in it. Since his childhood, Davros has been warned about the mutants who can breathe underwater. He's heard that they wait beneath the surface for the shadow of a boat to pass overhead, then they leap out and drag hapless sailors to their doom.

Davros and Elwyn have to walk for a little while to find the ferryman, who is waiting by his wooden boats, skimming stones into the water.

'Will you take us across?' Davros asks the back of the man's head.

He turns and Davros sees that his face is covered in lesions. One of his eyes looks cloudy. *A 'muto'*, Davros thinks. The word his mother would say with a shudder whenever she referred to those mutated and scarred by radiation exposure. When he was a child, the Kaled government rounded them up and exiled them from the city. Most of them, he's heard, eke out what living they can outside the dome.

The ferryman shakes his head and holds his hand out for money. Elwyn rummages through his pockets and produces a little hand-sewn change purse. But Davros gets there first, with a couple of silver coins that glint like pearls in the twilight.

The man offers them a weather-beaten wooden boat, and two oars.

'Can you row?' Elwyn asks.

'Of course not,' Davros scoffs. Elwyn sighs and takes both the oars.

'At your own peril.' The ferryman's voice is a low rumble as he casts his eye across the water.

They make slow progress at first. Elwyn rows, and Davros scans the surface of the water for any signs of disturbance.

It gets harder and harder as the sun sets, though, and Davros reaches into his bag for the screwdriver. 'What are you looking for?' Elwyn asks, the strain from rowing evident in his voice.

'I can use it as a torch.' With the turn of a dial, he switches on its flashlight function, but in the beam of light he sees Elwyn's pupils constrict with terror.

'No!' Elwyn shouts. 'Switch it off!'

'Why?' But at that moment, Davros looks back at the water and sees disturbances across its surface. Bumps, and then – his blood curdles – hands!

Elwyn screams, dropping one of the oars into the water. A body emerges, then a twisted face with no eyes or ears. It reaches its scarred and pockmarked hands towards Elwyn's throat.

Davros' limbs unfreeze at the threat. He lunges forward and grabs the other oar. He aims one hard blow at the creature's head.

Just as he does so, Davros feels a vice-like grip on his own wrist. He works hard to shake it free, rocking the boat so violently that the two of them almost fall overboard.

Then, another arm at his ankle. Another monstrous face from the deep. In the blink of an eye, there are almost a dozen of them, their features nightmarish in the moonlight. The boys are going to die. They'll be dragged into the toxic lake and torn limb from limb. Elwyn is screaming, doing everything he can to kick the attackers off, but his wiry physique is powerless against them.

A thought flashes in Davros' mind, a beam of inspiration. With his free arm he fumbles for the screwdriver he dropped in his panic. His fingertips find its cool edges. The move is almost reflexive, twisting and activating it the way he's taught himself to through years of silent practice. A beam of light appears from its crystal, and lands on the face of the creature holding his wrist. It lets out a roar of pain and the air is filled with the smell of its burning flesh.

This seems to frighten the others. Davros aims the screwdriver at the one holding Elwyn, who releases him with a shriek of agony. Elwyn's face is moon-pale with dread, and he has tears in his eyes.

'That's right!' Davros shouts, wielding the screwdriver now like a weapon. 'Any of you want some more of this?'

More cries, this time plaintive, and the mutated people swim backwards. In a couple of seconds they've all slid back under the water, leaving Elwyn and Davros in harrowed silence.

It takes a little while for Elwyn to pick up the blood-spattered oar and begin to row again. When he does, Davros resumes his watch, staring at the still surface of the water, scanning the ripples for fingers, for twisted faces. Sometimes he thinks he sees them, and the hairs on his neck stand on end, but they're only ever shadows. The mutos have returned to the lake's silty floor, where they will keep a silent watch for someone else to devour.

Once Davros and Elwyn reach the water's edge, Davros helps his friend to climb out and on to the shore. It'll be a long night. They'll set up camp a couple of miles from here and take turns keeping watch.

'I didn't know,' Elwyn says the next morning, eyeing Davros pensively as he packs the screwdriver back in his bag. 'I didn't know it was a weapon.'

'Among other things,' Davros says. He'd altered it himself, increased the intensity of the laser, making it hot enough to burn flesh. 'It also opens and closes doors and amplifies sound waves and . . . What's wrong with you?' Elwyn looks as if he's about to cry; his eyes keep flitting back in the direction of the lake. 'They're only mutos.'

Elwyn's eyes flash at those words. '*Only?*'

'Yes, they're –'

'– don't say that word. They're living beings,' Elwyn says. 'They're like you and me. It's not their fault they've been sickened by the radiation. They're not monsters. They were banished and forced to live like animals. I feel sorry for them.'

'Well . . .' Davros is already growing tired of this line of conversation. He's happy they made it out alive and keen to travel as far as they can before sunset. 'Be that as it may, they were going to kill us.' Then, with another glance at his friend, 'Oh, for Skaro's sake, Elwyn. What are you still so upset about?'

'I've taken a vow of peace,' he says. 'I've promised never to kill or hurt anyone.'

Davros is taken aback. He's heard of 'peace activists', although only ever in contemptuous whispers. His father described them as cowards or agitators. But this new information makes some sense of Elwyn's character. There is an inherent peacefulness about him – a gentle lilt in his voice – and Davros remembers the tender way he handled a dead bird they came across on their walk.

'You're a –' Davros almost doesn't want to say it, for fear some alarm will ring and his friend will be arrested.

'– peace activist.' Elwyn nods, looking at Davros defiantly.

'But if you get conscripted into the military –'

'I could be thrown in jail for the rest of my life.'

'And you think that's worth it?'

Elwyn gestures around, his motion encompassing the lake, the mountains, the whole planet of Skaro. 'Look at what war does, Davros. If we don't find a way to end it, we'll push everyone into extinction. In a thousand years, alien archaeologists will pick over the ruins of our cities and try to piece together what happened.'

The thought strikes Davros. He's only ever imagined either the Thals or Kaleds winning the war. Never the dire stalemate Elwyn describes. *Everybody* losing.

'But it doesn't have to be that way,' Elwyn implores. 'Maybe it won't. Not if you end the war as I believe you can. You will.'

It occurs to Davros now that this is why Elwyn has been willing to risk his life to go on this perilous mission. His friend's eyes are on fire with a kind of . . . faith. In him.

Davros reels. Catches a glimpse of himself as the man Elwyn dreams he will be. A man who will change history. A man worth dying for.

'I want to,' he surprises himself by saying it. He wants it to be true.

The ancient city lies in a valley between two mountains. To reach it, they must scale a precarious path up one side, and then down the other. The way is perilous, taking them up through the tropical air into a cooler, more rarefied atmosphere. Elwyn is a better climber than Davros has expected: his weather-worn sandals and nimble hands easily find purchase on the sheer cliff faces they scale, and he rebalances almost reflexively when he takes a wrong step.

Davros' heart is in his throat the entire time. Coming down the far side of the mountain, they encounter a narrow passage and Davros leads the way. He takes a wrong step and his foot flies out from under him. There is a sickly swoop in his stomach as he realises he's going to fall. That he'll tumble to his death among the rocks below. But then a vice-like grip is on his wrist. Surprising strength. 'I've got you,' Elwyn promises.

The sun is setting when they finally come upon the ruins of an ancient city. Stone pillars and sculpted archways, crumbled roofs and empty windows revealing the insides of houses. Mosaic floors scattered with dust or hollowed-out bones. Tangled vines strangling columns. Whoever lived here has long since vanished.

It is a strange and terrifying sight. Like looking into the dark eyes of a skull. A glimpse of death, but on an awful scale.

'I don't want this for us,' Davros says honestly. He imagines his own home in ruins. Floors churned up by tree roots, everything returning itself to the ground.

'This doesn't have to be our destiny,' Elwyn replies.

The last Dal – according to Elwyn – lives in the ruins of the city temple. When they find her, she is sitting on a throne-like chair, her eyes closed. Davros thinks she's dead upon first glance. Moths have spun nests in her floor-length white hair and there are cobwebs at her shins. But her eyes snap open at their approach. They are the same deep purple as Elwyn's. She looks as if she has survived alone for a thousand years. Davros wants to ask what science or sorcery is behind her longevity, but he's too frightened to talk.

Elwyn bows. Davros is late to follow suit. Elwyn says something in a language Davros has never heard spoken, only read in the *Book of Predictions*. They're speaking too quickly for Davros to follow. The woman replies and Elwyn translates, 'She says she knows why you're here.'

'You told her I want to see my future?' Davros asks.

'She says to warn you that everyone who glimpses their future is changed forever.'

'Yes,' Davros says. He's come this far. 'I want to be changed.'

The woman says something else which Elwyn doesn't translate and then gestures for Davros to step forward. He does so, walking on to the fissured stone under her feet, and then, at her gesture, he kneels.

She says some more words, very quietly this time, her eyes closed. Then, finally, she places her hand on his forehead.

It clutches him like an electric shock. Pain radiates from her hand to his skull and Davros cries out. When he opens his eyes, though, he realises he's blind. *What has this witch done to me?*

But then the vision comes into resolution. Several. It's as if his life is flashing before his eyes. He sees his own terrible face, now as deformed as those of the mutated creatures in the lake: sightless eyes, cruel smile. The Dark Lord of Skaro. The creator of the Daleks. The monster who ends the war by wiping out everyone on the planet.

'No!' Davros screams, leaping back, the puckered rock grazing his arms, almost kicking the woman off her seat with his motion. 'No!' he shouts again, rubbing his eyes as if to get the stain of this image out of them.

'I don't want it!' he shouts. 'That's not the man I want to be.' Elwyn looks pale. Has he seen it too?

Then, recovering his senses slightly, Davros steps forward. 'Give me another vision. A better one.'

'It doesn't work that way,' Elwyn says.

'But . . .' Davros is devastated, confused. 'That is not the sort of greatness I aspire to.' He wants to be like Elwyn: peaceful, good. 'Please,' he says to the woman, on his knees now. 'Give me another vision! A different future.' He's tempted to grab her hand and see if he can take one from her.

The woman only closes her eyes, muttering something ruefully.

Elwyn translates. 'You can't change the future.'

Heavy with despair, the two boys make their way home in the darkness. Elwyn is despondent. Changed.

'You don't believe it, do you?' Davros says, working to make his voice sound lighter than he feels. But he can't get the woman's vision out of his head, or the idea that this might all be some trick. Who was she, really? A muto? A Thal deceiver?

'I've been thinking about the story you told me when we were walking,' Elwyn says, 'about the man that you said you met when you were younger. The man who came from the future?'

'Right.'

'Well, what if . . . what if, because he lives in the future, he knows the sort of person you'll become? What if the reason he hesitated when you said your name was because he was frightened?'

'Why would he have saved me, then?' Davros asks, hating this.

'I don't know.' Elwyn looks at his feet. They're walking down a particularly precarious slope, and, in the dark, it's difficult to see where the ground might suddenly give way. It's dangerous to travel at this time of day but neither of them wanted to spend the night in the city. 'Maybe he's a bit like me. I wouldn't want to let even my worst enemy die.'

'Rather one person die than millions.' But then Davros shakes the thought away. Elwyn stays unnervingly quiet for a long while. 'Maybe,' Davros ventures, 'maybe it's actually that man's fault. My life was changed forever, set on some other path *because* of meeting him. I definitely wasn't as fascinated by science or invention until the sight of him inspired me to pursue it.'

Elwyn's eyes are dark with a new resolution as he remembers the visions. 'I thought you were a good person.'

'I am!' Davros says, wounded.

'I believed in you.'

'I didn't *ask* for your belief,' Davros hisses.

They walk in silence for another couple of minutes, Elwyn leading the way, only the moonlight illuminating their path. The ground is unsteady here, rocks skittering and toppling like shingle. One wrong step could be disastrous.

'If you were a good person,' Elwyn says finally, 'you would leave the city, live a solitary life in the wastelands.'

'No!' Davros' voice echoes through the mountain pass.

'If you leave then none of this will come to pass. You won't create those monster robots. You won't kill everyone on the planet.'

'No,' Davros says, his chest growing tight. It makes him sick to hear this – this litany of future crimes. 'I can be good *here*. I can change things *here*. I could choose peace like you. Refuse to join the Military Youth. Fight for an end to the war. Maybe that's why that man saved me, so I can do just that.'

'No.' Elwyn's jaw is tight as he stops walking and turns to Davros. 'A good man, a peaceful man would leave now and never return.'

'Never,' Davros says. They stare at each other, rage and fear prickling off both of them. Davros thinks suddenly, regretfully, *I've never had a friend before.* He considers the journey back with some misery. Imagines the days walking with this boy who suspects he's capable of so much evil. Can he bear it? And in the years after, even if the two of them never speak again, Elwyn's eyes will be watching him from somewhere, waiting to see if it's true, if he really is the monster they say he will be. The thought makes Davros sick.

Elwyn leans forward, maybe to shake Davros' shoulders, to press his point further. Maybe to hug him, as he sees the hurt in his friend's eyes. Davros will never know. Reflexively, he steps aside, so Elwyn is unbalanced for a moment, and his foot slips.

Davros leaps forward to catch him, and, just in time, his palm meets Elwyn's cool wrist. A flash of terror in those prescient purple eyes. 'I've got you,' Davros says, but Elwyn doesn't seem to believe him. Davros can feel his own balance slipping as he struggles on the precipice, his body and his mind wrestling against conflicting desires.

'Don't . . .' Elwyn says as if he can see it too – his own white hand thrown up against the darkness, a scream, his fall.

Davros almost doesn't realise he's let go until he has. And then, blood pounding in his ears, he shouts his friend's name into the void. Snatches the blackness as if he could undo it. His own voice, heavy with grief, echoes back up to him. Then silence, for a while, as he lies on the hard rock.

It was an accident, he tells himself a couple of times to soothe the beating of his heart. Tragic. *I did everything I could,* he imagines telling . . . who? No one knows either of them is here. Elwyn had kept his mission as secret from the few members of his family as Davros did.

It could be, he thinks now – the thought appealing to him – *as if none of this ever happened.* There are only three people on the planet who know what his future looks like. Two now, and Davros will probably never see the woman again. His muscles relax and he lets himself exhale. Davros realises that he's free to forget all about it. The whole unhappy encounter. The awful vision he saw.

He can live another life. He can choose something different.

Davros gets up, reaches for the screwdriver in his bag, twists the dial and turns it into a flashlight, to illuminate the way home. While he walks he considers what was said: 'You can't change the future.' And then he laughs out loud, his voice resonating off the old stones.

What neither of them understood is this: Davros can do anything he wants.

MURMURATION

MARK GRIFFITHS

'*And that was the latest number from those fresh-faced troubadours John Smith and the Common Men, and isn't it just a totally terrific toe-tapper? Mmm, digging that sound, boys! And now to take us up to the news . . .*'

Sarah Jane Smith clicked off her tiny transistor radio, slipped the device into her overcoat pocket and slumped back into the creaky deckchair, glowering. A long, shuddering sigh escaped her lips. The air inside the dilapidated shed was calm and musty, the restful hush broken only by the distant tinkle of birdsong. But her blood was still frothing with rage.

Crocus Pinker.

Just thinking of her classmate's name made Sarah groan with frustration and annoyance.

Crocus Pinker was the leader of a gaggle of girls in Sarah's year. They patrolled the corridors of Caterham School like vultures, alert for the smallest oddity. A slightly unconventional hairstyle, a pair of heavy and unflattering glasses, last year's threadbare jumper patched for another term, a sprinkling of pink pimples on a chin. Any deviation from the norm by a pupil would be pounced upon by Crocus and her crew as evidence of their owner's complete drippiness . . . and mocked mercilessly. Wherever they roamed, they left a trail of tears and snot in their wake. Had these girls bumped into Genghis Khan himself one morning break, Sarah mused bitterly, they would have reduced the great Mongol warlord to a squirming mass of shame in seconds with a few well-chosen quips about the cut of his imperial robes.

And the worst thing? Crocus wanted Sarah to join her gang. She'd been badgering her about it for weeks. Evidently, she had sensed in Sarah a strong personality – perhaps even a potential rival – and wanted to absorb her into her band of followers. It was the eternal dilemma, thought Sarah: bully or be bullied.

She knew it would be wrong to hook up with Crocus and her mob. And yet . . . she had to admit, there was something darkly thrilling about the idea. Those girls had *style.* And they had power – or at least were as near to power as fourteen-year-old schoolchildren ever came. They swept along the hallways like a tightly drilled army unit in pigtails and sandals, unstoppable, laughing. Crocus could be superbly witty in the cruel ways she put people down. (Once, to Sarah's horror, she asked Kitty Browning if she could borrow her best dress because her parents were planning a garden party and needed a marquee.) But surely the most sensible – the *safest* – course of action for Sarah was to join her gang? Wasn't it?

Sarah let out another groan. She was mightily sick of this dilemma, which was why in recent days she had taken to sneaking out of the school grounds at lunchtime and holing up alone in this derelict shed about half a mile away, on a disused allotment. Here at least – among the cobwebs, old fertiliser bags and other junk – she could be certain not to encounter Crocus Pinker.

Absently, she nibbled at her thumbnail and stared blankly out through the shed's cracked and filthy window.

What to do? What to do? What to do?

Suddenly, there was a noise. It was a distant electric throbbing, like the juddering of some vast motor. Sarah listened, her thin brows furrowed, as the sound rose and fell unsteadily in pitch. Humming. Chittering.

It was like nothing on earth.

The sound grew louder and a shadow, deep and impenetrable, moved across the window of the shed, briefly blotting out the grey November light. Heartbeat quickening, Sarah hauled herself from the deckchair and peered uncertainly through the grimy window.

A huge flock – no, a *cloud* – of starlings was buzzing and thrashing through the air above the allotment. A vast black mass like a gigantic ink stain on the white page of the overcast sky, the flock swooped and dipped over the scrubby grass, its shape constantly changing. The air overflowed with the birds' sharp cries and whizzed and hissed with the beating of uncountable pairs of wings.

Sarah watched, transfixed, all thoughts of Crocus and her gang swept from her mind. It was one of the most beautiful things she had ever laid eyes on. The flock whipped and undulated through the air as if it was a single huge organism, playful and free as a dolphin. She laughed with delight.

There was a word, Sarah knew, for this kind of enormous gathering of starlings. One of those funny collective nouns, like a conspiracy of ravens or a murder of crows. She had seen a table of them at the back of one of the fat dictionaries in the school library.

Murmuration! That was it. A murmuration of starlings.

And it was a fitting word, too, because the noise of the countless darting, whipping birds seemed to Sarah to contain within it the murmuring of a million mysterious voices. It was a strange, inhuman chanting, like a demonic choir or the midnight whisperings of witches.

Twisting, forming and re-forming, kneading itself like dough, the murmuration continued its ceaseless dance overhead. Sarah noticed a man in thick winter clothing and wellington boots standing on the edge of the allotment, as enthralled by the starlings' dizzying display as she had been. His breath formed tiny white clouds. At his side, straining on a lead, was a thin and nervous-looking greyhound, clearly spooked by the thronging birds.

The murmuration seemed to sense the man's presence and drifted lazily towards him through the air, apparently curious. Its constant chittering diminished to a low hum, as if the flock was gathering itself for some new purpose. The greyhound began to bark fiercely. Unperturbed, the immense cloud of birds hovered over them, its form shifting slowly from one abstract blob to another – until it finally settled in the unmistakable shape of a human skull.

Sarah gave a silent gasp.

The vast floating skull leered down at the man. Then its jaws gaped open, and it dived towards him with terrifying speed.

Sarah watched in horror as it swallowed the man whole inside its mass of writhing birds. The screeching and chittering of the starlings intensified to a deafening triumphant roar, drowning out the man's terrified cries. For a few grisly seconds the enormous floating skull actually appeared to *chew*. And a moment later, a single twisted wellington boot fell from its mouth and plopped gently on to the grass.

The greyhound gave a yelp and sprinted away across the allotment, its lead trailing.

Inside the shed, Sarah's blood froze. What in the name of holy flipping heck had she just witnessed? They were only normal starlings, weren't they? The little speckly things you saw hopping along the ground in car parks and suburban gardens.

Eyes fixed on the skull, Sarah backed away slowly from the window. Her elbow brushed a stack of terracotta plant pots perched on a rusty metal table, sending them tumbling to the floor with a crash.

At the noise, the skull whipped round, tilting slightly to one side, as if listening. Slowly, it began to drift towards the shed.

Panic bloomed in Sarah's stomach like an icy flower. Half the old shed's roof was missing and the structure would offer, as far as she could determine, zero protection from a murmuration of blood-crazed starlings. Heart thudding, she yanked open the door and sprinted out into the chilly afternoon air, frantically scanning the landscape for cover. The allotment backed on to the gardens of a row of narrow terraced houses, separated by a low chain-link fence. She could easily hurdle that and try to get into one of the houses through its back door. But what if it was locked? What if the homeowner wouldn't let her in?

She risked a glance back over her shoulder. The floating skull was hurtling through the air towards her, buzzing, screaming; its empty eye sockets seeming to blaze with inhuman hunger. Sarah gritted her teeth and picked up her pace.

What else was there nearby? A graffiti-daubed bus shelter. A low clump of anaemic-looking bushes. A patch of waste ground dotted with fly-tipped rubbish.

She spotted a yellowing fridge, its door hanging open on one hinge. A couple of rain-sodden mattresses. Some broken chairs. A battered-looking old police box . . .

A police box?

Weird. With its reassuring blue solidity, the police box stood out from its drab surroundings. Funny that she'd never noticed it before on any of her outings to the shed. Must be a new arrival, she thought. Would its doors be open? They had better be. Or she was toast.

The noise of the murmuration was almost deafening now. Sarah was half convinced she could feel the skull's hot breath on the back of her neck. Arms outstretched, she vaulted over the smelly mattresses and jammed the heels of both hands against the doors of the police box. They opened easily with a friendly creak. Pulse hammering in her head, she raced inside, spun on her heel and slammed the doors shut, resting her forehead against the frosted-glass window set into one of the doors. Outside, she heard the murmuration roaring in frustration, the thousands of seething, screeching starlings surging around the wooden box, cheated of their prey.

Breathing heavily, Sarah turned slowly around. Her nose wrinkled and a look of utter confusion spread across her face.

She should have been standing in a dingy wooden kiosk, barely five feet square. Instead, she found herself in a gleaming white room with circular-patterned walls. It was a space impossibly – *insanely* – big to fit inside an ordinary police box. At the centre of the room stood a complicated-looking hexagonal control panel covered in chunky buttons, levers and winking lights. Behind it stood a very tall man with a tangle of thick, curly hair. He wore a tweed coat, and an extremely long multicoloured scarf was wound around his neck. In fact, so preposterously long was this scarf, thought Sarah, that it would have made just as much sense to say that *it* was wearing *him*.

The man looked up. He appeared surprised to see her, but not displeased.

'Hullo, Sarah Jane!' Then he smiled.

It was like the sun coming out. Despite the horrific turn her day had taken, Sarah was filled with the sudden wondrous conviction that things might work out after all.

She still fainted, though.

Sarah's eyes snapped open. She found herself sitting on the floor of the impossibly large white room, her back to the wall. Her nostrils were under assault from noxious fumes wafting from a small glass vial the tall man with the scarf was waving under her nose.

'Yuk! What's that?!'

'Swerdlixian smelling salts,' the man said, laughing. 'Intriguing aroma, isn't it?' He dropped the vial into the pocket of his tweed coat. 'You'll be right as rain now.' He extended a hand and helped her to her feet.

'Smells like boiled liver,' said Sarah.

'That, Sarah, is because it's made from the boiled liver of the Swerdlixian marsh-pig.'

Sarah snatched her hand away. 'You did that before. Used my name. How do you know who I am?'

'I thought you might ask that. I'm called the Doctor, by the way.'

Sarah folded her arms. 'Big deal. I've had a bellyful today, mate, I don't mind telling you. First man-swallowing starlings, then impossible rooms hiding inside old phone boxes. And now a total stranger in the world's longest scarf knows my name. What's going on? Did I fall asleep in double maths this morning?'

The Doctor rubbed his chin. 'Let's see if I can't offer some explanation, shall we? And forgive me if I gloss over the details somewhat but time, as you must appreciate, is of the essence.'

'I'm all ears. What are you a doctor of, anyway?'

The Doctor flashed a set of pearly whites that would have made the Cheshire Cat envious. 'Oh, most things. Now, let's see. Those starlings are acting so peculiarly because they've been possessed by a non-corporeal being known as a Tononite.'

'I'm not sure that counts as an explanation,' said Sarah, 'because I'm even more confused now.'

The Doctor chuckled. 'The Tononite is a creature from another dimension.'

'What?' Sarah started to laugh but the noise died quickly in her throat. 'You mean like an . . .' She had to force the word out. 'An *alien*?'

'Precisely.'

'Gosh,' said Sarah simply. *So aliens are real?* That was a big thought. Almost too big to fit inside her head. She suddenly felt very cold. Her fingers and toes were tingling. 'I wish I had something clever to say right now but that's all I have. Gosh.'

The Doctor beamed. 'Perfectly respectable response. Shows you appreciate the gravity of the situation.'

Sarah nodded mutely. She could feel the urge to say *gosh* again but fought it off and tried to think of an intelligent question to ask. What had it advised in the *You Can Be a Journalist* book her Aunt Lavinia had given her last Christmas? *Always ask open questions: Who? What? Why? When? Where? How?*

'How did this thing get here?'

'Good question,' said the Doctor. 'It entered our dimension by creating a rift in space-time. The Tononite is a being of pure information with no bodily form of its own. A literal bad idea. It can only *be* by taking on an existing physical structure – the way a computer program exists only in the operations of the machine's circuitry. Or a symphony exists only as notes written on paper.'

'And this Tononite thing has taken control of that murmuration of starlings?'

'Indeed. The flock of individual creatures has become a single deadly organism.'

'Huh. Sounds like Crocus and her friends.'

'Like who?'

'Never mind.'

'Anyway, it requires a lot of energy to keep a flock of thousands of starlings going. And unfortunately a human being offers the perfect high-protein snack.'

'I saw,' said Sarah. 'That poor man.' She thought with a shudder of the way his mangled wellington boot had fallen from the skull's mouth. 'So where do you fit into this? Is this your job? Finding aliens?'

'Well, I'm more of a keen amateur these days,' said the Doctor, 'but that's otherwise correct. I tracked the Tononite here from the far side of the Glimmerous Vacuum Cataracts in my TARDIS.'

'Of the . . .? In your . . .?'

The Doctor nodded at the hexagonal console. 'This old thing. It can travel anywhere in time and space, you know.'

Sarah laughed nervously and steadied herself against the wall. 'Of course it can. Which I suppose means you're not from Earth either, are you?'

The Doctor's eyes widened mischievously. 'Not remotely!'

'Any of those smelling salts left?'

'Ha! I think you're coping admirably, Sarah. Particularly for one so very young.'

Sarah stuck a hand on her hip. 'I'm fourteen and a half, for your information. I'm no baby. And there you go again. How come you know me but I don't know you? What's the story there?'

'Because we haven't met yet. Not officially.'

'I don't understand.'

'I'm afraid that's all I can say about the matter,' said the Doctor. He picked up a strange-looking gizmo off the control panel – a weird lash-up of brightly coloured wires and circuits – and began to tinker with it. 'I know that must sound aggravating but sometimes the universe throws these little annoyances at us and we have to just accept them and get on with our day.'

'Fine,' said Sarah. 'Be all cryptic. See if I care. How do we deal with this Tononite thingy, then? Is this phone box equipped with missile launchers or what?'

'I'm afraid *we* won't be dealing with it at all,' said the Doctor. '*I* will. You will stay here in the TARDIS.'

'What? Just stand about like a lemon while you have all the fun? You're joking!'

'No point risking both our lives, Sarah. The future needs you. I may prove rather more dispensable.'

'What?'

The Doctor grinned. He seemed to have twice as many teeth as a normal person. 'Oh, just being cryptic again. I'm afraid a tendency to spout irritating statements is one of the side effects of time travel. Can't be helped. Now, let the dog see the rabbit.'

He twisted a dial on the console and a panel slid open on the wall, revealing a large rectangular screen. It showed a view of the allotment outside. Drifting through the air above it could be seen the murmuration of starlings, still in its skull formation.

'And there she blows. It ought to be slightly sluggish as it digests its elevenses, so now would be an excellent time to disrupt it.'

'Why is it shaped like a skull?'

'A common technique of psychic entities. The idea is to terrify its victims. Apparently flesh seasoned with fear is so much sweeter.'

'*Ugh*,' said Sarah. 'I wish I hadn't asked you now. How are you going to disrupt it?'

The Doctor held his wires-and-circuits gizmo aloft proudly. 'With this white-noise generator. White noise is composed of all audible sound frequencies just as white light is a mixture of all visible colours. One of those sound frequencies should be perfect for jamming the starlings' telepathic link.'

He yanked a lever on the control panel and a set of white double doors whirred open. A wintry breeze whistled in from the allotment outside. Then he reached into the cavernous pocket of his tweed coat, drew out a shabby broad-brimmed hat and screwed it on to his thick mop of hair.

'Back in a mo.'

'One more question, Doctor.'

The Doctor paused in the doorway. 'Yes?'

'Isn't that scarf terribly annoying for a man who goes about fighting alien monsters?'

'Oh, I don't know. Came in rather useful on Kastria.'

'Where?'

'Wait and see.' He winked and disappeared through the thick double doors. With a whir, they closed behind him.

Sarah sighed and stared around the strange white room, noticing an old wooden hat stand lolling in one corner. This

Doctor bloke had odd taste in clothes. Not bad, necessarily. Just . . . odd. With a faint smirk, she imagined herself strolling back into school some time that afternoon. '*Late, am I? Oh, sorry. You see, I was hanging around in a spaceship while a strange alien man dealt with a rampaging creature from another dimension and I rather lost track of time. I know what you're thinking – same old excuses!*'

She watched on the TARDIS scanner screen as the Doctor edged his way along the chain-link fence towards the murmuration. Every few paces he would stop to make some adjustment to his . . . what did he call it? White-noise something. The vast flock of birds was coasting lazily some distance off and appeared not to have noticed him.

As she studied the screen, she saw one end of the Doctor's long scarf snag on a broken fence link. Half a second later it pulled tight and jerked him backwards with unexpected violence, half throttling him, and he dropped the white-noise generator, which fell on to the scrubby ground and broke into several pieces. Frantically, the Doctor scrabbled all around him for the parts of his machine.

'You ridiculous man,' muttered Sarah. 'You're going to get yourself killed.'

She turned to the console. Which control had operated the double doors? She tried a few knobs and switches at random, praying the TARDIS didn't have a self-destruct function, until with a loud whir of motors the double doors swung open.

'Doctor!'

With nimble fingers, Sarah unhooked the Doctor's unfeasibly long scarf from the fence. He was so intent on collecting the fragments of his device that he had barely noticed he was snared.

'What are you doing out here?' he hissed. He kept one eye on the murmuration, which appeared still not to have noticed them. 'I told you to stay inside the TARDIS!'

'Lucky for you I didn't, mate. I did say this wardrobe choice was a bit risky, didn't I?'

'Forget the scarf. The white-noise generator's broken. Without it we have no way of disrupting the Tononite's hold on those birds.'

'It just occurred to me . . .' said Sarah.

'Yes?'

'I know where you might be able to get hold of another white-noise thingy.'

The Doctor's eyes widened. 'You do?'

'Yes. I –'

A terrifying howl from the sky drowned out the rest of her words. The air filled with the frenzied susurration of thousands of starlings.

'It's seen us,' said the Doctor. He scrambled to his feet, stuffing the fragments of the device into his pockets. 'We need to get to safety.'

They turned towards the TARDIS but found the murmuration blocking it from view.

Sarah's heart lurched. 'Where now?'

'Anywhere's better than here. And probably best we don't dawdle. Come on!'

He grabbed her hand and the pair of them galloped away across the scrubby grass, the Doctor's scarf billowing, the murmuration gaining on them by the second.

'Is this other white-noise generator close by?' gasped the Doctor as they sprinted.

Sarah thrust her free hand into the pocket of her overcoat and pulled out her transistor radio. 'It's this. I read somewhere that the static you get between radio stations is the same as white noise. That's right, isn't it?'

The Doctor took the radio and grinned. 'Marvellous, Sarah! It's absolutely perfect! I just need a few seconds to boost the amplitude.'

He skidded to a halt and drew a slim cylindrical device from his pocket. He pressed it against the radio's loudspeaker and it emitted a high-pitched whine.

'Hurry up, Doctor!' cried Sarah. 'The birds are getting closer!'

She stared, frozen with fear, at the black, skull-shaped cloud of starlings careering through the air towards them. To her surprise, though, it appeared to be melting away and re-forming into – what? A strange machine-like creature with a single eye on a stalk and a pair of waving rod-like arms . . .

'What's it supposed to be now?' she muttered.

The Doctor didn't look up. He was too busy fiddling with the transistor radio. 'Probably picked some bogeyman from one of our nightmares. Don't let it trouble you too much, Sarah. Ah! We're in business!'

He clicked the radio on and a deafeningly loud burst of static erupted from its tiny speaker.

'Gosh, you really souped that thing up!'

'Cover your ears, Sarah,' said the Doctor. 'It's going to get a lot louder.'

Sarah did as she was told.

The birds were almost upon them now, the air thick with them. The Doctor wrenched the radio's volume up to maximum and held the device aloft. The air shook with noise. It felt to Sarah as if she was standing next to a jet engine, her every atom vibrating madly. She risked a glance at the murmuration.

Something odd was happening to it. The sharp edges that defined its shape were blurring. Individual birds were breaking away from the flock and flying off in random directions. The entire huge black shape was dissolving away to nothingness before her eyes like a sugar lump in hot tea.

'It's working, Doctor!'

Like drifting smoke, the murmuration dispersed into the afternoon air, clumps and strands of birds thinning out to invisibility. After a few seconds, there was not a single starling to be seen in the sky.

The Doctor clicked off the radio and the roaring wall of white noise abruptly stopped. Sarah removed her hands from her ears. The silence was almost overwhelming.

'You did it!'

'*We* did it, Sarah. If it wasn't for you I'd be starling food.' He handed her back the radio. 'Come on.'

They set off for the TARDIS. Overhead, a gap appeared in the dreary clouds and a pale November sun showed its face. Somewhere, a single robin trilled. Walking beside the Doctor felt somehow very right and comfortable to Sarah. Despite having only just met him, she'd sensed an instant connection with this traveller in space and time. It was all very *companionable*.

'So what's become of the bodiless beastie? The Tononite?'

'Gone,' said the Doctor. 'They're rather flighty creatures. A slap on the nose like the one we've just given it and it retreats through its space-time rift like an eel into its crevice. It'll think twice before trying its luck again in this universe.'

They had arrived at the TARDIS. The Doctor turned to face Sarah. There was a strange, melancholy smile on his face.

'This is goodbye.'

Sarah forced a laugh. 'Not going to whisk me away in that thing to the far side of the Glimmerous Vacuum whatsits, then? I wouldn't mind. It's double home economics this afternoon.'

'Impossible, sadly.'

'And you're going to let that stop you because . . . ?'

'Ha! On this occasion I have no choice.'

Sarah studied the words inscribed on a panel set into one of the blue box's doors, trying not to meet his eye.

POLICE TELEPHONE

FREE

FOR USE OF

PUBLIC

ADVICE & ASSISTANCE
OBTAINABLE IMMEDIATELY

OFFICERS & CARS RESPOND
TO URGENT CALLS

PULL TO OPEN.

'I-I'll never forget this afternoon,' she said quietly. 'I'll never forget *you*. This is the most extraordinary . . . the most amazing thing that's ever happened to me.'

Again there came that melancholy smile from the Doctor. Sarah didn't like it as much as his big, toothy grin.

'I'm afraid you will forget, Sarah.'

She gasped in mock outrage. 'Oh yeah! Meeting space travellers and alien creatures is normal, is it? Barely worth a mention in the school magazine.'

'It's not that. You see, now the Tononite has left our universe, the space-time rift it created will heal. This timeline we're experiencing will be erased and it'll be as if these events never happened.'

Sarah's voice cracked. 'But they *did* happen! They *did*! How do you expect me to go back to my normal existence after this? It's not fair!'

'Just be yourself, Sarah. There's no more important job in the universe.'

She clutched his arm. 'Will *you* remember?'

The Doctor smiled again and this time it was the real thing, bright as a beacon. He winked. 'Until we meet again for the first time.'

He pushed open the door and went inside. There was a bizarre grinding, trumpeting sound and the TARDIS faded slowly away.

Sarah laughed in astonishment. 'Yes,' she said to herself, grinning. '*Of course* it does that.'

Sarah blinked. A loud wash of white noise was pouring from the speaker of her transistor radio. It must have drifted out of tune. She switched the device off and slipped it into the pocket of her overcoat. She shivered, suddenly cold. How long had she been sitting here in this deckchair, zoned out? A glance at her watch told her she had better make her way back to school. It was double home economics this afternoon, as if the day hadn't been boring enough already.

As she folded the deckchair and placed it neatly against the wall of the rickety shed, a thought came to her with striking suddenness. It was the clear and overpowering conviction that Crocus Pinker could go and jump in a lake.

THE BIG SLEEP

DAVE RUDDEN

'Seeker Va'stra,' High Judge Acrocan said, a dark and amused finality in his voice. 'Your time has come.'

Va'stra didn't smile at the joke. She just looked down at the datascale gleaming between them – a little disk of silver circuitry bright against the cracked, worn leather of the desk. Outside the High Judge's window, the upper districts of the city of Vambrace sweltered under red skies. There was a fire burning somewhere. Another riot, perhaps, not yet crushed by Acrocan's forces. She'd seen the prefects arming themselves for combat on the way in.

'You're not pleased?' Acrocan asked. Even now, he could read her. Acrocan had been her mentor ever since she was a lowly cadet, and he was hunting thieves and murderers through the neon caverns of Vambrace's lower levels. She'd been assigned her own first hunt in this very office – a petty smuggler whose name she was ashamed to say she could no longer recall. It was here she'd sobbed after the Rudoku Conspiracy, when she'd thought about quitting the order and it seemed there was no good to be found in anything.

And it had been Acrocan who had convinced her otherwise. *In this job,* he had said, *good is prey to be hunted. It doesn't come easy and it doesn't come to you. You have to find it yourself.*

Va'stra owed this ancient, bent-backed reptile a lot, and it was a little sad to see the hard-won awards and certificates on the walls packed away, as if even this office too was old and shedding its scales.

'It's just strange,' she said finally. Va'stra hadn't accessed the datascale yet, but she knew exactly what it was – an electronic key containing her name, her rank and duty as a Seeker of Truths, and then a string of digits and letters that marked her place in Vambrace's vast Hibernation Complex. She had seven days from accessing to decide what would be done with her home and belongings, and then she would step into a stasis pod and go to Sleep for a hundred years.

They were calling it the Crisis, though Va'stra always thought the word was too dramatic. Long-range sensors had picked it up at first – a rogue asteroid that was going to brush past the Silurian homeworld, dragging away its atmosphere, leaving the whole world lifeless for a century.

Many solutions had been discussed since then. The military talked about deflecting or destroying the threat. The priesthood railed against the idea of disturbing the natural order. Civilians disbelieved it, or fled into space on great ark ships, or turned to – or on – each other.

It had been a busy few months, until the leading Science Advisors submitted what would become known as the Response. They would abandon the surface. They would build Hibernation Complexes. The Silurian race would wait out the disaster in stasis, safely asleep, frozen in time until the atmosphere returned.

'It's a damned relief, is what it is,' Acrocan said, leaning back in his chair. He seemed smaller every time she visited now – his head crest greying with age, the skin tightening back from his lips until it felt like she saw too much tongue and fang. 'I can't wait to get mine. Get some sleep!'

He barked a laugh, and now Va'stra smiled, because she didn't like to think about him laughing alone. Laughter in this job, she had been told, was important.

And then Acrocan looked out of his window, and his smile disappeared.

'I know why we are the last to get them. The peace has to be kept while all remaining citizens take their places. But soon the only reptiles left awake in the city will be the blood-gangs, and that isn't the Vambrace I want to live in.'

'You say that like you're happy to leave it to them,' Va'stra said.

'I am,' he responded simply. 'The blood-gangs are already at war. Rebel groups from the northern jungles have been spotted within a day's march of Vambrace. When the complex is full, the defences will come online, and they'll be yesterday's problem. The old world is ending, Va'stra. We're all going to wake up in a new one. A better one, I hope.'

'It's only a hundred years,' Va'stra said. 'I think we'll probably still be in this one.'

'You're too young to be that cynical,' he said, and activated the window shutters, closing out Vambrace with the click of a switch. 'A fresh start is just what our society needs. A way to leave behind the old traditions and build something beautiful.'

His voice softened.

'I know it's a lot to take in,' he said. 'Go home. Meditate. Let things sink in.'

'I still have some paperwork to –'

Acrocan laughed again. 'Paperwork? Va'stra. As serious as when you were a cadet. It's all being closed down. Set in stasis, like us. Just take the last few days off. Visit old places. Get your head straight for the Big Sleep. That's the best thing you can do right now.'

'You're right,' Va'stra lied, and picked up the datascale. 'Thank you.'

The city of Vambrace was a hot and smoky warren far deeper than it was tall, delving four full miles into the Earth's crust to drink deep of its geothermic heat.

Only the richest districts – Apex, Goldenrod, the Spirebreak where Acrocan's Prefectory stood – protruded above ground level. Underneath was a gigantic cavern that held the city proper – neon-red and silver against the black stone, connected to the surface districts by a spiderweb of walkways and transit tunnels.

Va'stra watched it grow larger through the window of her travelling cage, the wrought-steel sphere plunging down from cavern roof to floor, along the Topaz Line, so fast it felt like she was falling. She never grew tired of this view, but more and more she looked at it like a hunter examined a crime scene: marking the healed scars and the new wounds, looking for clues as to what might have led to this chaos. As if it wasn't being announced from the cage-mounted screens over and over again.

++ *The greatest challenge of our time* ++
++ *Have you considered our new stasis cubes for pets?* ++
++ *Scientists say less than a century's sleep* ++

The Topaz Line was one of Vambrace's main thoroughfares, and the looping path it took across the cavern gave Va'stra ample opportunity to note the marks of the Crisis. Normally the line was packed at this hour, with groups of sullen miners or bright-clad youths with chains swinging between their crest spikes. Now, she was the only Silurian in the rattling cage, and the only signs of life below were the smoke and flames of gang fights and riots.

The only thing that did please her was the green. The jungle had only reluctantly allowed Vambrace's construction in the first place, and now everywhere Va'stra looked she could see it reclaiming that which the Silurians left behind. Vines were curling down the cage's tubing. The dark tunnels the transit cage occasionally swept through were lit by luminescent fungi, and roots could be seen in the bedrock on the other side of the glass.

We'll have a lot of work to do, Va'stra thought. *When we wake back up.*

Her home was a modest affair – just a set of basalt cubes with light strips across the ceiling and walls. It was intended for a family – a perk of her rank as Seeker of Truths – and so she had one extra cube that she used as her office, with hooks on the walls for armoured bodysuits, the civilian gear she wore rarely (if at all), and the sword that gleamed from its rack like a shard of cut glass.

There wasn't much indication of a life well lived. Va'stra knew that. There were no souvenirs or keepsakes. No signs that a person did anything here but sleep. She ate at the mess hall in the Prefectory, or grabbed things on the run, because running was what she did.

Va'stra was a Seeker of Truths. Prefects kept the peace, High Judges judged criminals, but Va'stra's job was to hunt. She was an investigator. A tracker. *Curative, not preventative.* The others under Acrocan's command tried to prevent crimes, but Va'stra found those who committed them, and did what had to be done to make them stop.

The hunt was not everything to Va'stra, but it was most things. She didn't see a problem with that. And yet, it still felt strange to know that all of this was going to be put away.

She sat underneath her wall-mounted work terminal and began skimming through communications. No personal messages – her sisters had gone to Sleep weeks before, and her few friends had done so as well. She scrolled through security announcements and city-wide safety updates:

> ++ *Wild pack of Deinonychus detected in sector one nine.*
> *Capture-and-release teams deployed . . . ++*
> ++ *New hostilities erupting between Redcrests and Brandish*
> *Maw blood-gangs at Junction Emerald – all citizens to*
> *avoid . . . ++*

Va'stra was not a soldier. It wasn't for her to keep the peace in that way. And yet, it hurt her to see the chaos. It was not the way of the Silurian to hide their wild nature. There was no strength in pretending you were better than the beasts with which you shared the world. Strength came from accepting your wildness and turning it to good use. Silurians didn't hide what they were, but they did control it. And now all of that was going away.

Acrocan's words came back to her.

It's all being closed down. Set in stasis, like us.

And then something caught her eye.

The case had been filed just an hour ago, by someone in the Gutworks – the lowest level of Vambrace, a warren of tunnels where the poor and the poorer-than-poor worked the mines and factories that now churned day and night for the Response. The Gutworks had never been safe even in the best of times, but now law only existed in pockets.

She checked who had filed it. Ah, yes. A youngblood, barely two years on the job. Eager, too, when their comrades were no doubt planning to sleepwalk their way into Hibernation. Eagerness did not buy you friends. Va'stra could have told them that.

As serious as when you were a cadet.

Va'stra switched off her terminal and went to get her sword.

'Thank you for coming all the way down here.'

Va'stra could smell the newness on Prefect Third Class Eliphraz. He must have been barely out of the nest when the Crisis was announced. And now, here he was, a skinny little reptile in too-clean clothes, nervously pacing the morgue as she gently lifted the first blanket back from the body underneath.

'You sent this case to me specifically,' Va'stra said. Seekers were usually assigned by High Judges, not requested by prefects on the ground. 'Why?'

'You weren't my first choice,' Eliphraz said, and then cleared his throat. 'I mean, I submitted a request through the proper channels, but there's been no response.

And I know Seekers like you have dealt with blood-gangs before.'

She looked at him sharply then, though she should not have been surprised. Prefects loved stories, and there were plenty of stories about Seekers. They worked alone. They answered to no authority but their own, and that of their High Judge. Prefects protected, but Seekers hunted, and that hunting sometimes led them to work alongside, rather than against, criminals – in the service of tracking their quarry.

'And you're investigating this alone?' Va'stra said eventually. 'What about your squad? Your commander?'

Eliphraz sighed. 'Right now, most of my comrades are focused on getting their datascale and going to Sleep before a bullet finds them instead.' He eyed her a little bashfully. 'Don't tell them I said that.'

Va'stra didn't say anything. It made sense – why rush to file those reports? Why rush to clear out cases that were all going to be put in stasis anyway?

Why are you here, then?

'Who was he?' she said, pulling the sheet back further. 'Do you know?'

'Veddick Mor,' Eliphraz said. 'Record as long as my tongue, and –'

He indicated the red-tattooed head crest.

'No wonder they're up in arms,' Va'stra said. 'The Redcrests don't let the death of one of their own go unpunished.'

'That's the thing,' the young prefect said. 'He wasn't, any more.'

'What?'

'I mean he was clean,' Eliphraz said. 'Hadn't run with them in a decade. I think he was managing a kitchen in the Gutworks for those who didn't have the money for food.'

That suddenly made the whole thing sadder. Va'stra could see the long scars of blade-fights across Veddick's arms, the scar tissue around cheek and eye. And all old. All healed. The life he had been living for the last few years had not been violent.

And someone had killed him anyway.

'What makes you certain it's not a grudge from the bad old days?' Va'stra asked, laying the sheet back in place. 'Redcrests make enemies. They're good at it.'

Eliphraz blinked. 'Does that mean we don't investigate?'

Va'stra didn't have an answer for that. Instead, she asked to see the next body, and the next, and the one after that.

Eight criminals, some reformed, some decidedly not, had been hunted down and slain in the last two weeks. Never the same way twice, which in itself was a message. The blood-gangs out there liked to sign their work, kill in a way that would be recognisable. Here, though, it was poison, it was falls, it was sabotaged transit-lifts.

It seemed that the goal was not to send a message. It was simply to take their lives.

'There's always a connection,' she said to Eliphraz, before she left him worriedly pottering around that rundown morgue. 'Find that, and we find our quarry.'

Back at her terminal, she accessed the Prefectory's database using a far higher level of access than Eliphraz's.

Veddick Mor had been busy in the weeks before he died. His personal communications lay open before Va'stra. She couldn't access much more than the subject heading of each message without a High Judge's sign-off, but one phrase kept coming up again and again and again.

The shipment.

'What shipment?' she said aloud. 'Drugs? Weapons?'

Three of the dead criminals were on the recipient list. Had Veddick fallen back into his old ways? Was *the shipment* some new scheme or old score? Was that why he had been murdered?

Does that mean we don't investigate?

'Computer,' she said, 'search all active case files for recent mention of a shipment. Missing, stolen, en route, anything at all.'

The terminal's voice hadn't changed. Of course it hadn't. But something about it felt more dull and tired, as if even it was winding down.

++ *Information not found.* ++

'Explain,' Va'stra said. She knew there were cases there. She'd filed many of them herself.

++ *Information deleted in preparation for Societal Hibernation.* ++

Va'stra hissed in frustration. Of course. All of society was shutting down. That was the simplest explanation for the murders as well. With law and order failing – no, not failing, just sleeping – it was likely some criminal was taking their chance to hunt down their enemies.

It would have been inaccurate to say that Va'stra made her decision then. In truth, she'd made it the second she'd contacted Eliphraz instead of finding her stasis pod and letting the whole thing rest.

'There is no new world without fixing the old world,' she said to herself, and reached for her sword. 'You have to hunt the good.'

The Gutworks. A miles-deep maze that hung under the cavern of Vambrace like the tentacles of a poisonous jellyfish. Nobody really knew the full extent of the tunnels. There were the mines, obviously – the dark, dank holes where precious minerals fed the engines of empire. Only the miners had mapped those, and only because there was wealth at the bottom.

But for every mining shaft there had to be access tunnels for maintenance, and vent networks for power and air, and then there were just the caves – a thousand sub-caverns and pit-camps where the poor and forgotten slept and ate and dreamed of the sun.

That was where Va'stra walked now, in armoured bodysuit and hunt-mask – its heat sensors painting the darkness red.

There was a system for things like this. Places where messages could be left. The blood-gangs all hated each other, and they hated the High Judges, but that didn't mean they didn't *talk*. There were deep places where they even mingled, on treaty days and ceasefire festivals, though it felt like those times were long gone.

It was part of her training to leave Vambrace sometimes and make her way out into the jungles beyond. Va'stra did it more than most. There was something pure about it. The hunts there were not complicated. No bureaucracy. No paperwork. You hunted and you hid and you stayed one step ahead of the creatures hunting you. Some of the newscasts – those that still ran, anyway – talked about how Vambrace had become a jungle, but the fact was it hadn't. In the jungle, everyone would have just done what they had to do to survive.

She made her way through moisture-slick tunnels that neglect had turned into flowerbeds. Once or twice, she heard echoing gunfire, but it could have been miles, or the width of a wall, away. The acoustics made it impossible to know.

Eventually, she reached a crossroads – eight tunnels feeding into a circular cavern hung with chained platforms and walkways, a handful of grav-lifts drooping where their batteries had nearly given out. Va'stra had always thought of it as some sort of rusty heart: for its shape, and the tunnels leading away like arteries.

In the centre of the chamber was a four-storey tower of iron scaffolding. Its original purpose was forgotten, but now it bristled with dozens of wreaths – gempenny and deadfinger, dagon's thistle and acrimony. All flowers from the jungle outside, and all deadly – tributes to those gang members who had died.

Va'stra scaled the side of the tower easily, taking care not to dislodge any of the flowers. She'd leave her message here. The Redcrests would find it. And if someone was killing them over this shipment, they might even tell her what it was.

'Va'stra?'

It was Acrocan on her comm-link. He sounded even more tired than before, and a little harassed.

'High Judge?'

'What are you doing? I'm getting updates that you haven't handed in your weapons or uniforms. That you're requesting archived files. Your Sleep is in five days. Why aren't you preparing?'

He didn't sound harassed, she realised. He sounded angry.

'Eight murders in the Gutworks,' Va'stra said, easing herself over the railing and on to the third floor of the structure. 'I can upload the files when I get back. Someone is targeting blood-gang members. There's talk of some shipment – of what, I don't know. This might be why the blood-gangs are at each other's throats.' It suddenly occurred to her that if she found the culprit, they might stop fighting each other.

'So?'

Va'stra stopped. A chain was swaying up ahead. In a draught? Had a grav-lift dropped a few feet?

'Repeat, sir?'

'So what, Va'stra?'

Her voice echoed around the rusty heart of the chamber, so acid it surprised even her.

'Someone has murdered eight Silurians, *High Judge*. Shouldn't we find out why?'

Acrocan's voice was hard. 'Eight criminals.'

'That doesn't mean they should die,' Va'stra snapped, and then composed herself. 'Apologies, High Judge.'

A long silence.

'I know you don't want to leave work on the table, Va'stra. That's admirable. Really, very admirable. But you are not going to solve this in five days, and, even if you did, there may not be anyone to bring the case to a court. Hells, there may not even be criminals left to try. Everyone's getting their datascale, Va'stra. Everyone's going to Sleep. You should think about whether you want to do the same.'

The link went dead, and Va'stra realised he was right. She had five days left in this world. Was this dark tunnel where she was going to spend them?

She pulled off her mask to look around one last time, and then something wet hit her cheek.

Va'stra was moving before the second drop of saliva landed, flinging herself over the railing and down the three-metre drop to the second-floor deck with blade out. A moment later, the entire scaffolding structure rattled to its core as a fully grown Deinonychus crashed down where she had been standing moments before, leaving dents in the corrugated floor.

There were myths about Deinonychus. There were myths about all the dinosaurs with which the Silurians shared their world. Brachio the Old Father, Therapod Saint, the souls of the dead living on in the dinosaurs that walked and crawled and flew. It was half the reason Va'stra and others like her went out and hunted among them, in the hope their spirits would mingle and live on in the jungle's heart.

But you didn't hunt with Deinonychus. They hunted you. They hunted everything. They were smart and cruel in a way that animals shouldn't be. This one's long head pivoted on the S of its neck to stare at her first with one eye, then the other, as if it was giving her a theatrical view of its serrated teeth. The long sickle claw on its foot *tap-tapped*, *tap-tapped*, like a timer ticking down.

They ate you alive, if they caught you. Va'stra remembered that from her lessons. And, as a low growl sounded behind her, she remembered they usually hunted in packs.

Va'stra was ready for the second Deinonychus as it came – pelting out of the shadows, tail out and high, head low and straight, so its whole body formed an arrow seeking her heart. It gathered itself and bounded at her in a leap that crossed the six metres between chamber floor and platform like it was nothing. Va'stra threw herself sideways, the whole structure swaying, and the thing chittered what might have been a laugh.

Va'stra didn't even think about fighting. She rolled under the second-floor railing, a heartbeat ahead of snapping jaws, and fell hard to the decking below. The two dinosaurs barked at each other – one going left, one going right, closing off her options with military precision.

Is this because of the Crisis? she wondered, because wondering about that was better than wondering if she was going to survive. She'd escorted Silurian scientists out into the jungles before so they could tag dinosaurs with non-lethal control nodes that kept them from wandering into Vambrace. Had those controls been shut down? The city was being abandoned to the hungry jungle . . . was it now inviting the predators in too?

All the way down here?

She got to her feet and bolted across the chamber floor, turning the movement into a somersault that just managed to outpace the first creature as it grabbed for her. She spun through the air, slid *down* its back with a rasping brush of scale on scale, and then twisted as she landed so the second missed her with a sweeping rake of its claws.

The predators stopped snickering then. It was chilling – now they were silent, all intent and hunger, one growling to distract her while the other prowled out in a wide circle so it could come at her from her blind side. Misdirection. Distraction. It was how she and Acrocan had worked, back in the day, and it was still effective now. Va'stra was unable to plan or gain ground, too concerned with keeping both attackers in her view.

Predator behaviour. Which made sense. But what didn't make sense, what itched at her own predator's mind, was why they were *here?*

Plenty of easier places to get prey. Plenty of prey between here and the jungle, even.

And they had come to her.

Misdirection. Sometimes, you might not survive a hunt. Va'stra had always wondered if she'd know that time when it came to it, and what she would do if it did.

Now, she knew.

With a flick of her wrist, she disarmed herself, sending her blade spinning upward in an arc of silver. The eyes of both Deinonychus couldn't help but follow it. That was what predators did.

And then Va'stra's right foot caught the first dinosaur in the snout.

There had been nothing in any of Va'stra's training about engaging a fully grown Deinonychus in hand-to-hand combat. Presumably, the recommendation was not to do it. But Va'stra didn't intend to win this fight.

She just needed to –

The surprised animal honked, rearing back to clutch at its snout, and Va'stra slid underneath it and got a good look at the base of its throat.

There was a little scar, and a blinking red light. Va'stra stared at it for a fraction too long, and then jaws closed on her boot.

A third Deinonychus dragged her bodily out from under the first, and only her armour stopped her from losing her foot. It wrenched its neck and flipped her, and suddenly Va'stra's face was in the dirt, pinning her in place. Hot breath blasted across her neck. Saliva rained down, turning the dust around her to blood-red mud.

No sleep, then, she thought. *Acrocan will be disappointed.*

And then suddenly the weight was gone. The Deinonychus landed beside her, head lolling, eyes rolled back in its skull. Its arms and legs kicked spasmodically, and that claw frantically *tap-tap*ped as if signalling for help.

Weakly, she rose to her knees. Systems in her bodysuit were already stopping the bleeding from her back but she knew she'd be feeling the bruises for weeks.

'Eliphraz,' she rasped. The other two dinosaurs were down as well, all lolling and shivering. 'I told you not to follow me.'

'He didn't.'

Va'stra looked up. The gantries and podiums above were crowded with figures. No two of them were the same – clad in dinosaur hide and chain mail, bone quills and flamboyant headdresses. All were armed, and all wore masks. Not as high-tech as hers but marked with crude runes and violent splashes of paint.

Every one of them had a spiked red crest.

'We did,' their leader said, and then raised his rifle and fired.

The skyline was burning.

High Judge Acrocan filed the last of his reports, resisting the urge to go to the window and work out *what* exactly was burning. The clouds were low over Apex tonight, billowing magenta and mauve where they were painted by the light of the fires.

That was how he thought of the city now. A painting. An illusion. The *real* Vambrace was underground – tucked away in the blue-lit cathedral of the Hibernation Complex like diamonds in velvet. Everything else was just a distraction. Acrocan was good at filtering out distractions. He'd been doing it a very long time.

Some Silurians spent the night before their Sleep with their families. Some indulged in wild celebration, despite the medical advice. Some visited their priestesses, or meditated, or obsessively checked their arrangements.

Acrocan hadn't done any of that. His family was here. He'd chastised Va'stra for it, but, really, there was nowhere else he'd rather be, right up until he closed his eyes.

He was about to call for his driver when a message came in over the comm-system.

'High Judge, this is Prefect Gotter, at Sentry Post 1C. We're under fire by unknown –'

Booms crackled over the link, eating the prefect's words. Acrocan heard the whip and crackle of beam weapons, frantic shouts as the sentries tried to repel the threat. Acrocan's fingers danced across the keys of his terminal, bringing up live images of the Prefectory. The blood-gangs – the Redcrests, the Brandish Maw. Even the jungle rebels.

All *cooperating.*

'High Judge!' Gotter's voice came again, low and urgent. 'There are too many of them!'

They know.

Acrocan did not waste a moment. He was out of his office by the time Gotter's tense request for orders became desperate pleas for help, and in the elevator by the time the link went dead. By the time the Redcrests had breached the Prefectory, he was out into the red darkness of Vambrace.

The old skills never left you, not really, and Acrocan had made a lot of effort to keep them sharp. He found his secret stashed armour, a pair of curved *dak* blades and a pistol with a full clip. Acrocan kept the Prefectory at his back, keeping to the shadows, making his way to a mostly forgotten set of lifts that connected Apex to a part of lower Vambrace a whole regiment of prefects wouldn't have braved.

Nobody saw him. Nobody heard him. But for the fires and the whooping alarms, as far as Acrocan was concerned the whole city may already have been asleep.

It took a little under two hours to arrive at the Hibernation Complex, and the sight of it eased the tightness in Acrocan's chest. In contrast to the weathered redness of Vambrace, the complex was a fortress of steel and blue light, set into the black basalt bedrock.

Many of the High Judges had demanded it be built in Apex or Goldenrod, somewhere *safe*, but Acrocan had argued that the deeper it was, the safer it was from the Crisis, and they had layered enough defences into its perimeter that no gang would be able to scratch it.

Acrocan felt his scales prickle as he approached. The complex looked more like a prison than the most important building in Vambrace, an impression underlined by the dozens of wall-mounted cannons that activated as he neared the gates.

++ PRODUCE DATASCALE FOR ENTRY, CITIZEN ++

The voice blared from hidden speakers before repeating itself in a variety of Silurian languages. Acrocan held his datascale up, and, with a click, the gates opened.

The inside of the complex was just as functional. Offices, more security checkpoints, a reception area where, in busier times, attendants would have led whole families down to their stasis tubes. Now, the white-painted corridors were empty, the lights brightening as he walked beneath them and dimming again as he passed.

Acrocan's stasis tube was two levels down, between a set of tubes belonging to a miner family of eight and an instructor in ritual dance. It was all very equal. He'd chosen it himself. Too many of the elite had rigged the systems so that they were in areas close to the medical bays, or behind extra layers of defences. That went against the purpose for Acrocan. They were all in this together.

Besides, nobody would look for a High Judge down here if, somehow, the rebels and blood-gangs managed to get in.

The stasis tube hinged open as he activated it. They'd designed them to look like eggs. Reassuring to a Silurian – that was where they'd come from, after all. Acrocan threw his pistol in, and then looked down at his blades. He wasn't sure if he had room for them, but no hunter could ever rest easy when unarmed.

Well. *Sacrifices have to be made –*

'Good evening, High Judge,' Va'stra said behind him, and then her blade was at his neck.

'Va'stra?' Acrocan didn't try to move. He knew how fast she was. Faster than him, certainly. But soft. He knew she would not hurt him and wondered if she was aware of that herself. 'Thank the gods. I thought the Redcrests –'

'The Redcrests have their own grudges,' Va'stra said evenly. 'I'm . . . helping them with their inquiries.'

'*You're helping them?*' Acrocan spat. He couldn't help himself. 'They're prey. We hunted them!'

'We brought them to justice,' Va'stra hissed back. 'That was the point of the hunt. All deserve justice. All are protected by it. All are subject to it. Even you.'

His blades were still in his hand.

'How did you know?'

'I didn't,' she said. 'Not at first. The blood-gangs fighting over some mysterious shipment? Retired criminals falling back into bad old habits? That's nothing new. Nothing to go on. And then the Deinonychus found me in the tunnels. At first, I thought it was random. A failure of the control nodes that keep predators out. Just another symptom of the Crisis.

'But if that was true they'd have just killed whatever they could find. That's what Deinonychus do. And instead they found their way into gang territory. As if they were hunting. So I checked their throats. Neural control nodes still active.'

'A malfunction,' Acrocan said carelessly, subtly adjusting his grip on his blades. 'You're risking your career over a malfunction?'

'The Redcrests saved me,' Va'stra said. 'And I asked them what the shipment was. What could be causing all this trouble. What was plunging the whole city into unrest.'

'And what did they say?' Acrocan asked. He felt the old predator in his heart wake up. 'So I can rest easy.'

Va'stra's voice was soft. 'They said a High Judge had blocked their shipment of datascales.'

'They wouldn't have added anything to the new world we're building, Va'stra.' One quick reversal of the blades, a backwards stab. It might not even be fatal. Acrocan didn't want to kill her. She was good at what she did. 'They didn't add anything to this one either. Why do they deserve a second chance in our bright future?'

'You were going to leave them to the Crisis,' Va'stra said. 'No datascale. No Hibernation. That's murder. And that's not even counting the people you *did* murder. Did Veddick find out what you were doing?'

'Nobody cares what happens to some criminals, Va'stra,' Acrocan said smoothly. 'Veddick, though . . . he was reformed. A community leader. If he'd gone public, people might have listened.'

Just another fraction of an inch . . .

Her mask crackled with an incoming message, and Acrocan took his chance. The blades spun in his hand with the speed of a much younger warrior, and Acrocan slammed them back into where he knew she would be. Va'stra gasped –

And Acrocan looked down in disbelief at the blade tip poking from his chest.

'You really are very fast,' he said, and then suddenly his knees didn't work.

Va'stra didn't waste a moment, and Acrocan didn't resist. He was too bemused by the pain to question why she was placing him in the stasis tube, folding his limbs up around him like he was a hatchling being tucked into bed.

'I'm quite sure I missed all your vital organs,' she said briskly, and it was only because he knew her that he could tell she was crying. 'But, just in case, the stasis tube should keep you alive. The Redcrests have the evidence they need from your office. All your hunts. All your victims. What you tried to do.'

'No magistrates,' he burbled. 'No jury left awake.'

'Not yet,' she said, and activated the tube. 'Sleep well.'

'What did you do after that?'

It was late. Jenny was curled up under a rug, her head on Vastra's chest, and Vastra absently plucked at her hair, marvelling at its softness. *Hair.* Honestly, Silurians didn't know what they were missing.

'I worked,' Vastra said. 'I worked with Eliphraz, and the Redcrests, and any gang or prefect who would have me. I found out how he'd used his influence and contacts to block the blood-gangs getting their datascales, and when I was sure the case was watertight I uploaded it to every single database I could access, so that the first issue on the desk of every Silurian magistrate would be the prosecution of the murderer High Judge Acrocan.

'And then I tried to help Vambrace. Acrocan was determined to get his better world, so I decided to get it for him. The Crisis was still coming, I couldn't change that, but I could try and get as many of the reluctant and the fearful to trust the process as I could. I missed the seven-day deadline on my datascale, and then a second, and then a third, and it was only on the day that asteroid entered our atmosphere I found my own tube and I went to Sleep.'

'And they're all still Sleeping,' Jenny said. 'Millions of years later. Do you . . . do you ever think about waking them?' Her smile wavered a little. 'Start that better world?'

'I don't know how,' Vastra said honestly. 'It would be the work of a lifetime, and that's not my purpose. I am a Seeker of Truths, and a hunter of criminals.' She leaned in and kissed Jenny's brow. 'And I've found the good in the world I have.'

DOCTOR JONES

FARIDAH ÀBÍKÉ-ÍYÍMÍDÉ

I t was on a cold Wednesday evening in the middle of January that Martha Jones's life would change forever.

Triggered by a sequence of unbelievable events laid out by the mastermind that some call the universe and others God, her life would be altered completely and irreparably as a result of the actions of a meddlesome Time Lord.

Though she would never know of this fact.

Martha had been seated at the dinner table, attempting to conjugate a particularly troublesome set of French verbs, when it happened.

'Ow!' a voice yelped behind her.

Followed by a series of gently hushed profanities.

Martha turned to see her mother at the kitchen counter, biting her lip and clutching her hand hard.

'Everything OK, Mum?' Martha asked, concern itching at her. It was very unlike her mother to swear.

'I was chopping the carrots for the casserole and nicked my thumb,' she said, and inserted the sliced digit into her mouth.

Martha got up from her seat, abandoning her French homework, and headed towards the downstairs bathroom right by the kitchen.

'Where's the first-aid kit again?' Martha yelled, opening the medicine cabinet and scanning the shelves.

'Inside the red box, in the medicine cabinet!' her mother called out, her voice still muffled from her thumb.

Martha stood on tiptoe, still seeing no sign of it.

'It's not here,' she finally declared.

She heard her mother curse again, which only made her more worried.

'I bet your father took it when he was last here, said he got an injury from work or something. I told him to put it back, but when has he been one to listen –'

'Do we have any spares?' Martha interrupted, not wanting her mother to start going on again about how incompetent her father was.

It was a song she was all too used to hearing whenever she was around either her mum or her dad – and it had only got worse with the divorce. Her mum would complain about her dad's inability to do anything right, and her dad would complain about her mum's complaining and it would always result in the same thing for Martha.

A migraine.

'No, I think that was our only kit . . . but it's all right, I'll just put a paper towel over it and it'll be good as new.'

Martha stepped out of the bathroom and gave her mum an incredulous look.

'That's not how cuts work! You could get an infection,' she said, exasperated. She strode over to her mum. 'Let me see it.'

Her mother sighed, placing her hand in Martha's.

Martha examined the cut carefully. It was much deeper than she would have liked.

A smaller cut could be washed and monitored for the night, but this . . . this needed a bandage at the very least, and maybe even stitches.

'I'm heading out to the shops. They should have one of those simple emergency kits.'

Her mother shook her head. 'It's honestly not as serious as it seems, and, anyway, don't you have French homework to finish?'

Even more reason for Martha to leave the house.

'French can wait, I suck at it anyway. This break is doing me a favour.'

'You're in Year Eleven now, GCSEs are just around the corner . . . I'm honestly fine, I don't want to be the reason you get a D in your French exam.'

Martha went to grab her coat. 'Trust me, this will definitely not be the reason I fail French. It's not like I'm taking it for A level; I don't get why I have to waste time on it.'

That made Martha's mother's eyebrows shoot up, her bleeding thumb suddenly forgotten. 'A levels?' she asked, finding it hard to mask the hopefulness in her tone. 'You've picked your options?'

She hadn't.

Picked them, that is.

But her mum had still perked up at the mention of A levels.

It hadn't been long since Martha had announced, at a family gathering, that she wasn't so sure if school was for her after all. And was considering leaving at the end of Year Eleven and going straight into work.

'But why? What's wrong with getting a good education first?' her mother had pestered her, voice rising with alarm.

'*The only things I'm any good at are biology and maths, and I don't need a degree to become an accountant,*' *Martha had replied.*

'*Be a doctor, then. You like taking care of people.*' *Martha's older sister Tish had chimed in with a shrug.* '*You love all those medical shows, you're good at science and you'd look good in those blue scrubs.*'

Martha rolled her eyes at that. '*You really think I could be any good at medicine? I can barely look after myself. And anyway, medical school takes forever. How will I have a life or get married or even have the time to do all the other things I love doing –*' *Martha started but was interrupted, by her father this time.*

'*Your Aunt Pam is a doctor, isn't she? She got married.*'

'*You mean the same Aunt Pam who's now divorced and unemployed and lives with all those smelly cats in Grandma's basement?*'

Martha's mum shot her dad a look. '*Thanks for the help, Clive,*' *her mother said with a sigh, before turning back to Martha.* '*Please, just consider A levels, for me? And if you really decide they're not for you, we can look at sensible alternatives, OK?*'

Sensible alternatives, *aka something that would still involve her completing her A levels and then university.*

Her mother was never this understanding. It had all been an act to show her father that she had become the reasonable parent who knew exactly what she was doing. And so, Martha was fully aware that it was either agree to do her A levels despite not being good at most of the subjects she was expected to be good at, like languages and literature and physics, or quite literally die.

'Yes, well, kind of. I think I might do maths, biology and chemistry – I'm actually pretty decent at chemistry, so why not?'

This made her mother's lips stretch into a smile.

Martha could see the relief on her mum's face.

'And university?' she asked cautiously.

Martha nodded slowly, zipping her coat up. 'Maybe. But, anyway, my priority right now is your thumb. I'll be right back with some supplies.'

'Thank you, *Doctor Jones*,' her mum said, as Martha exited the house in one swift motion, feeling the vibration of the door as it swung back and closed with a loud bang.

Then she stepped out into the cold, dark winter evening towards a future where nothing would ever be the same.

The corner shop was cold and dank and had this green-blue tinge that made her feel like she was in one of those post-apocalyptic movies.

When she stepped inside, the bell above the door chimed noisily, alerting the shopkeeper that he had a customer.

* *Face her mother's true wrath.*

He gave her a polite smile, so she nodded and smiled back at him awkwardly.

She scanned the small shop, trying to work out where they might keep household things like first-aid kits, but couldn't see past the sea of food tins and bottles of years'-old apple juice.

Martha heard a low humming.

In the corner, examining a particularly battered-looking tin of tuna, was a tall stranger in a dark coat. She watched him for a few moments, then went back to searching the shelves.

'Can I help you?' the shopkeeper finally asked, after watching Martha struggle.

She looked at him, and was taken aback by something in his expression.

No . . . not his expression. His face.

She hadn't noticed it before.

How *weird* he looked.

She didn't mean *weird* in a rude way, just that he was strange. His face was strange. It looked like he was simultaneously young and old. Like he could be her age or in his late fifties.

But it wasn't like he'd used some kind of miracle skin regime. It was almost as if his face kept changing, shifting at first slightly, and then drastically, each time she blinked.

Martha felt something pass behind her, like a ghost making its presence known in a haunted house. But when the shop bell chimed loudly, indicating that someone had either left or come in, she knew it wasn't a ghost at all.

Possibly just the stranger she had seen before, leaving the shop.

'Can I help you?' the shopkeeper repeated, staring at her with a piercing dark-blue gaze and pulling her away from her winding thoughts.

Blink. He could be twenty-five.

Blink. He could be sixty.

Before she could open her mouth to speak and ask him about a first-aid kit, there was a bright flash outside the shop.

She winced as the light filled her eyes.

It was like looking directly into the sun.

What the hell is happening? She turned back to the shopkeeper, who had somehow got even weirder.

Though now the weirdness wasn't his ever-changing face itself, but the expression on it.

His eyes were wide, and he was clutching the table in front of him.

His back arched slightly, his chest billowing. His Adam's apple bobbed as he dry-heaved into the air.

Is he about to be sick? Martha hoped not. She couldn't stand the sight of someone vomiting. It made her feel sick too.

She held her breath and stepped back as the shopkeeper gagged once more. But instead of chunks of undigested food spilling from his lips, something worse came out. What seemed to be hundreds of tiny insects erupted from his mouth, spattering all over the counter, scurrying everywhere.

Some of the bugs dropped to the floor, others clung to the shopkeeper, dribbling down his chin and making their way to other parts of his body.

Martha wanted to scream.

But before she could do anything, before she could even breathe, there was a loud bang, followed by complete darkness, and she got the odd feeling that she was suspended in air – falling through space.

The scream died on her lips as the shop vanished from the street. Forever.

At first, there was nothing but a deafening silence.

No white noise. No distant sound of humming. Or the gentle patter of bugs scuttering about.

Nothing.

And then, all at once, as if someone had turned on all her senses with the flick of a switch, she felt everything.

Light filtered through, followed by the sound of screaming and the thud of her back against solid ground. A searing pain shot through her arms and legs at the impact, and her skull connected with the tiled shop floor.

She pressed her fingers to her scalp, and felt warm wet blood oozing out between them.

Martha winced, squeezing her eyes shut as she waited for the pain to subside, before opening them again.

She blinked a few times, taking in her surroundings.

Where am I?

What happened?

She had been in the shop talking to that creepy shopkeeper . . . then bugs . . . and darkness.

She looked up, half expecting him to be there, standing over her with tiny insects crawling out of his mouth and roaming over his body. But when she did a quick scan of the shop, there was no one.

She was alone.

Now Martha noticed the state of the shop: shelves collapsed, shards of broken glass on the floor . . . and a pile of small blue first-aid bags on the ground nearby.

She sat up and reached out for one of the bags and then for a small bottle of vodka that had fallen off a shelf but remained intact. She unscrewed the bottle slowly, then opened the first-aid kit and placed the alcohol on one of the small medical pads inside, then dabbed at the cut on her head with it, wincing at the stinging sensation.

She had learned at school that alcohol was a natural disinfectant. It would make sure the cut didn't develop into something more serious.

Martha then placed a plaster on the cut, hoping it was her only injury.

The screaming had now been replaced by chatter and shouts of alarm. The noise seemed to be coming from outside.

Her eyebrows furrowed as she pushed herself up gently, pocketing the alcohol and the first-aid kit. She ambled towards the door, blinking to focus her vision.

Martha didn't notice it at first.

The thing that had obviously changed about her surroundings.

It wasn't until she opened the door that the realisation, along with the shock, suddenly hit her.

This *wasn't* her neighbourhood.

She was surrounded by towering trees, in the middle of some kind of forest.

She looked back at the shop, and then turned to face the small crowd of horrified-looking strangers staring at her and the building with wide eyes.

Someone let out a cry which was followed by more screams.

'Where am I?' she whispered to no one in particular.

Which is why she was surprised to hear someone answer.

'Salem, Massachusetts,' a strangely cheerful voice said, in what seemed to be a northern accent.

Martha whipped her head round and was surprised to see the odd humming stranger standing before her.

'M-Massachusetts? As in America?' she asked.

'Yes,' he replied, as though what he had just said made perfect sense.

How could she be in America? Weren't the flights from London seven hours long?

She didn't remember being on a plane or travelling for hours.

Was it possible that this strange man had kidnapped her, given her some sedative and taken her to the airport himself?

Is it possible that what felt like seconds was actually hours spent travelling?

Martha remembered the time her dad had his appendix removed. He'd said when they'd put him under it had felt like only moments had passed, when in reality he had been asleep for hours.

So maybe it was that.

Maybe this man *had* drugged her.

But that didn't explain the corner shop . . .

She quickly backed away from him, and picked up a random stick from the ground, holding it up.

'Did you kidnap me, then? You know that's a crime. I'll report you,' she said, breathing hard. But when the strange blue-eyed man didn't seem fazed by her words, she decided she had to do something. 'I can hurt you, you know? I'm not afraid,' she continued, this time throwing the stick at his head.

The onlookers gasped and she turned to them. For a moment she'd forgotten that she had an audience.

A bizarre audience, at that. They were all dressed in weird old-fashioned clothes and seemed like they hadn't had a shower in a while.

A man emerged from the crowd with a furious expression on his pale face.

He raised an arm and pointed his finger at her.

'Witch!' he exclaimed, and more gasps sounded.

Martha was even more confused now.

Did he just call her a witch?

'What –' she began but was interrupted by the angry man.

'Seize her!' he yelled, and two large men came hurtling towards her.

She had no time to escape. Before she knew it, the men were on either side of her. Grabbing her arms and carrying her away.

She struggled against them, kicking and fighting. But she was trapped.

As they dragged her away to a large old-fashioned wooden carriage in the middle of the path, she felt hundreds of fierce gazes burn into her skin.

Followed by the sound of people chanting, 'Witch! Witch! Witch!'

Why do they keep calling me that?

She turned her head back to look at the abandoned shop, standing displaced in the middle of the forest clearing, and noticed the strange man regarding her silently. His expression was unreadable.

And then she watched as he went back into the shop, leaving her to be dragged away.

Martha felt helpless and confused. Her thoughts whizzed around her brain at a million miles per hour.

Two thoughts were more prominent than the rest.

The first was that this had to be some eerie dream. One that just felt very real. Her mum did always say she had an overactive imagination.

And the second, the one that was most pressing even amid all the noise and her attempts to break free.

Who was that man?

After an hour or so, they arrived at a small village on the outskirts of the forest, where Martha was carried into a tall stone building and thrown into some kind of medieval jail cell by one of the burly fellows who had snatched her from the forest.

She had tried fighting them off, biting, kicking, screaming, but it was no use.

Martha was no match for them.

Maybe if she had paid more attention in PE, she wouldn't be here right now.

Wherever *here* was.

The cell doors closed, and she watched helplessly as one of the men locked it with a rusty key.

Then they disappeared down the hall, leaving her behind in the gloomy cell.

'What are you in for?' a soft voice asked in the dark.

Martha was almost certain the voice had come from inside her. But when she turned round she noticed a young girl sitting on a small wooden stool. She had the same old-timey clothes and dirty appearance as the people from the forest. Though she was much younger than anyone Martha had seen out there. Couldn't be more than twelve.

'I'm not sure,' Martha said.

The girl nodded. 'Probably witchcraft, if you're not sure. A lot of the uncertain ones get brought in for witchcraft.'

'Witchcraft?' Martha repeated, remembering the way the people had yelled *Witch* at her, as though accusing her of something.

But it couldn't be . . .

'But witches don't exist . . .' she continued, which only made the girl's eyes widen as if Martha had said something utterly unbelievable.

'According to the people in charge, they do, and the townsfolk agree – witches are real, they're dangerous and they should burn,' she replied, as though repeating words that had been seared into her memory.

And, from the look in her eyes, perhaps they had been.

The young girl winced suddenly, grabbing Martha's arm, grimacing at the slight movement.

'Are you OK?' Martha asked, looking down at her arm.

The girl shrugged. 'I think so.'

Martha noticed splatters of red staining the girl's small hands. She had a cut, or maybe something worse.

'Can I take a look at your arm?' Martha asked, remembering the first-aid stuff she had in her pockets. She probably had enough left over to help.

'S-sure,' the girl said.

Martha kneeled down slowly, releasing the girl's hand from her arm. She pushed the sleeve of her dress up a little, revealing a deep gash underneath.

'I'm just going to clean and bandage it, is that OK?' Martha said.

The girl looked confused but nodded anyway.

And so, Martha got to work. She poured some of the alcohol into the lid of the bottle and soaked a medical pad in the liquid before placing it on to the gash and wiping away the blood and dirt that had got inside.

Once it was clean enough, she grabbed a bandage from the kit and tightly wound it round the girl's arm, covering the gash completely.

'There, you should be good as new in a few days,' Martha said with a smile, which faltered slightly when she saw the girl's frightened expression.

'A-are you a healer?' the girl asked.

Martha's eyebrows furrowed.

'A healer?'

'Y-yes, I hear that the witches – there are different kinds. You just fixed my arm, so I figured you must be a healer.'

Martha shook her head. 'I'm not a witch.'

The girl didn't look convinced.

'Are you afraid of me?' Martha asked.

The girl considered her answer before speaking. 'They think I'm a witch too,' she said in a frightened whisper. 'That's why I'm here. So no, I'm not afraid of you.'

Martha blinked at her.

The girl was so young, barely a teenager. How could she be in here? How – *why* would people do this?

Who even believes in witchcraft any more?

She paused, turning over that question in her mind.

Her brain replayed the conversation she had with the strange man from before.

He had said that they were in America.

Salem.

Something about that felt familiar.

Martha felt the hairs on the back of her neck rise and her body go cold.

'What year is this exactly?' she asked, suddenly feeling on edge.

'1692,' a familiar voice replied from the darkness.

Martha's head whipped round as the strange man appeared once again, this time from the shadows.

'W-what?'

He looked at her with a perplexed expression. 'Didn't you hear me? I thought I was projecting my voice – I have been working on that –'

'1692,' she repeated in disbelief, interrupting him.

'Yes, I just said that,' the man replied.

'How – why –' Martha began.

'You're asking the wrong questions. It's not a matter of how or why, but who. That'll answer the why and the how, and, luckily for you, I know who it is.' The man stepped closer to Martha's cell and opened his hand.

On the skin of his palm was a tiny jar, and sealed inside, writhing around on its back, was one of the tiny bugs she had seen crawling out of the shopkeeper's mouth. Although this bug was a deep electric-blue colour, whereas the others had been the colour of dirt and bark.

'Hello, Peter, we meet again,' the man said, quite cheerily, to the blue bug.

Martha wanted to cry. This had to be a nightmare. She wasn't in America, nor was she in *1692*.

Witches weren't real.

Time travel wasn't real.

Nothing about this could be real.

But, as she blinked, her brain wouldn't wake her up.

It couldn't.

This was her reality.

'Can someone please explain what's going on?' Martha asked.

The man suddenly looked up at her. 'Ah yes, you see, I came to stop this evil time termite from wreaking havoc in the timeline and messing with the natural order of things, and luckily I was able to catch and neutralise him. I call him Peter,' he said, nodding down at the blue bug.

Martha was even more confused.

Evil time termite?

Timeline?

She had no idea what Mr Strange was on about.

'Mr . . .' she began, not knowing his name and waiting for him to fill the gap.

'Doctor,' he corrected.

'Doctor what?' she said.

'Just Doctor.'

She refrained from rolling her eyes. How pretentious was that?!

'OK . . . Doctor. That doesn't answer my question. I have no idea what any of that means.'

He *ahh*ed as though he'd just figured something out.

'Sorry, I forget humans aren't so well versed in all this. The shopkeeper, Peter, is the time termite.'

'The shopkeeper . . . is a bug?'

'A termite.'

She blinked at him. 'How does that explain anything? I couldn't care less if he was a beetle, I just want to know why I'm here.'

'Time beetles are very different creatures from time termites, I can assure you . . . but I digress. Peter, the shopkeeper, is an evil time manipulator who has the ability to multiply himself and take on a human-like form. I tracked him down to the corner shop, where he was posing as a shopkeeper. He probably ate the actual shopkeeper,' the Doctor said, tutting at the bug in his hand. 'And Peter here likes to mess with the fabric of time. He's the reason we're here, in 1692. I believe he uses his antennae to mess with the time waves, ultimately leading to the ability to travel to any point. I'm rather glad he brought us here and not to a more dangerous time like the age of *dinosaurs and sheep*.' He shuddered. 'He's usually kept in a cell similar to yours, in a different galaxy, but somehow he was able to escape. Luckily, I've got him!'

The Doctor grinned from ear to ear as Martha stared at him in absolute shock.

'Is he a witch too?' the little girl finally spoke.

Martha nodded slowly. 'I think so.'

'Hey, I'm not a witch. I'm a Time Lord. Two very different things.'

'OK, Doctor Time Lord –'

'Just Doctor will do,' he interrupted.

'OK, *Doctor*, how do I get out of here?'

The Doctor's eyes lit up and he grabbed something from his pocket that looked a lot like a pen or perhaps some kind of tool . . . like a screwdriver. Then he tapped the bars lightly and Martha watched as the cell door swung wide open.

'There, you just step on out and I'll return you to your own time at once.'

Martha felt relieved, but only for a few moments. She remembered the girl behind her.

'How about her? Can you let her out too?'

The Doctor turned to the little girl, and regarded her for a while.

'Was she accidentally brought to this time as well?'

Martha shook her head. 'N-no, I think she's from here. But she doesn't deserve to be locked up. She's an innocent kid.'

The Doctor looked between Martha and the girl, a grave expression appearing on his face. Like he was burdened by something greater than himself.

'I'm sure she is. I'm sure a lot of the people suffering here are innocent. These witch trials . . . they are unjust, and show a weakness in this world. Not in these women. I wish I could help her. But I can't.'

Martha did not understand this man at all. How could he agree that the girl was innocent, but then in the same breath suggest leaving her there?

'Why not?' Martha asked.

The Doctor sighed. 'The Salem witch trials are a fixed point. Removing them will alter the timeline and we can't afford that. Her being here is very important.'

'In English, please,' Martha said.

He looked up at the ceiling, like he was thinking of a way to translate all the seemingly nonsense jargon he had just uttered.

'I've never used this one before . . . but have you seen the film *Back to the Future*?'

Martha nodded slowly. She had watched it once with Tish and Leo.

'Well, the film is not at all accurate and has made humans entirely incompetent in space-time matters, but, anyway, remember what happened in that film when the boy went and snogged his mum?'

Martha nodded, understanding now. 'He started to disappear.'

'Exactly. If I change anything, there are an infinite number of future events that could be permanently altered. Even us being here right now could alter things completely. So we have to leave, before anything significant happens –'

'Hey!' a loud voice boomed from behind, as two guards approached the cell.

'Like that,' the Doctor said, gesturing to them.

The men were quickly approaching him, sizing him up.

But for some reason this Doctor person didn't seem all that fazed.

Martha watched him grab a small jar of the brown termites from his jacket pocket, take two out and then produce the same metal object he used to unlock the cell, twisting it about before throwing the bugs in the faces of the guards.

They stumbled backwards, and she watched in horror as one bug crawled up one of the first guard's nostrils, and the other bug disappeared into the second guard's eyeball.

It didn't take long for the two men to drop to the ground.

'W-what did you do to them?' the young girl asked, now pressed against the cell bars to get a better look.

The Doctor opened the jar again, pulling out another termite.

'Well . . . what was your name, again?' the Doctor said.

Martha felt bad. She had never even thought to ask the girl's name.

'Abigail, Abigail Williams.'

'Well, Abigail, Abigail Williams,' he repeated with a sad smile. 'I simply made sure they'd forget. It's like a deep sleep, and the guards will wake up unharmed. It'll be like nothing happened. Their lives will be the same as before.'

Abigail nodded, understanding. 'That doesn't sound that bad,' she said.

His eyes were glazed over. 'I'm sorry. It will be over before you know it,' he said, before placing a termite on the young girl's nose.

Martha watched as it burrowed its way into her nostril. Then Abigail Williams' eyes rolled back and she collapsed on to the mud, falling into a deep sleep.

Martha suspected that it would be the last peaceful sleep the young girl would have before she had to face her untimely fate.

It wasn't fair. None of it was.

She felt helpless. She wished she could've helped Abigail, and that the world wasn't so awful to young women and girls. Some things never seemed to change.

The Doctor dusted off his palms.

'Right, then, let's get you home.'

'You're not going to put one of those termites on me, are you?' she asked, stepping back into the cell. Suddenly, Martha found the bars more comforting than the prospect of the scary flesh-burrowing insect.

The Doctor raised an eyebrow. 'It doesn't hurt.'

She still wasn't all that convinced that he was telling the truth. 'OK, but how does it work exactly? Where does it go?'

'I programmed them to go into your brain, find your amygdala and eat away at the memory of this particular day.' He paused, looking at her horrified expression. 'Just joking. The termites will only be used to get you home, seeing as my usual mode of transportation isn't here. I'll erase your memories of this day myself – also a painless process, I promise. I will have to erase this from my own memory of course. Remembering the termites enables them to control the time period you're in, which can cause all kinds of problems, like corruption of governments, the alteration of fixed points –'

'Aren't most governments already corrupt?' Martha said.

The Doctor paused, considered her argument and then nodded. 'You have a point. I guess there's not much more the termites can do there . . . But, anyway, I promise no harm will be done to you or your brain, though I can't guarantee the same for Peter, as it will be his antennae that I'll be using to get us back.' Then he took out the jar and released two more termites on to his palm. He tapped them both with the silver pointed thing once again and the bugs lay still, no longer writhing about. 'Here, take one, and squeeze.'

Martha eyed the bugs nauseously. She suddenly felt like she was in the matrix being asked to choose a red pill or a blue pill. One that would change her life and the other that would end it. 'Why should I trust you? You could have programmed them to attack me for all I know.'

'Well, it's either stay here and wait for the guards to wake up and take you to Gallows' Hill to be hanged . . . or squeeze a bug and return home to your normal life. Your choice.'

Martha sighed. It wasn't much of a choice at all.

'You should hurry with that choice, by the way. This lot will wake up any minute.'

Martha slowly reached out to squeeze the bug, her face and stomach twisting in disgust.

'Good choice!' the Doctor said.

Maybe a countdown might help? she thought to herself.

Three . . .

Two . . .

One . . .

And then, like before, the world around her closed up, and everything went black.

*

Martha had always suspected that the world would end someday.

She just never thought she'd be alive to witness it.

When they'd first arrived in Salem, before she knew it *was* Salem, she'd wondered whether she'd ever see her mum again, or her dad, or Tish and Leo.

The thought of never seeing her family again was a painful thing.

Even more painful than French homework.

But now, as she lay in this vacuum of time, nothing was painful any more.

She would see her family again. Things would be better, back to normal.

The Doctor had made sure of it.

For now the day spent in Salem would roll off her and cease to exist in her mind.

Any initial unease she felt could be passed off as déjà vu . . .

'Ow!' a voice yelped behind her.

And Martha jumped at the unexpected sound . . . or maybe she did expect it. But wasn't quite sure why.

Martha turned to see her mother at the kitchen counter.

'Everything OK, Mum?' Martha asked.

'I was chopping the carrots for the casserole and nicked my thumb . . .'

Martha paused, looking around the room.

Why did she have the funny feeling that this had already happened?

'Again?' Martha said, laughing it off.

'What?' her mother replied.

'You seem to hurt yourself a lot these days. Let me get the first-aid kit,' Martha said, leaving her French homework and walking into the bathroom.

'Where is it again?' Martha asked, opening the medicine cabinet and scanning the shelves for the red box where they usually kept it.

'Inside the box, in the medicine cabinet,' her mother called out.

Martha stood on tiptoe, and at first she couldn't see any sign of the red kit, but then something small and square at the back of the cabinet caught her eye.

A blue emergency kit she hadn't seen before.

Weird.

'Found it!' she said, heading back to her mother.

'You're a star,' her mum said, reaching out for it.

Martha shook her head.

'I'll do it,' she replied, gently taking her mother's hand in hers. The cut was deeper than she would have liked, but the kit should help fight infection.

Martha disinfected her mother's thumb, then placed a bandage on it.

'There, good as new,' she said.

'What would I do without you, *Doctor Jones*?' her mother said. The word *Doctor* gave Martha that strange sensation again. Like her brain was reaching for puzzle pieces – for the answers to some great mystery she couldn't quite work out.

'I'm not a doctor, Mum . . . not yet, anyway,' she replied.

Her mum gave her a hopeful glance. 'Not yet?' she asked.

Martha nodded. A memory was itching at her, accompanied by a deep sadness she couldn't explain.

'I don't know, I think I'd like that. Healing people. Helping people. I think I'd be good at it.'

Her mum looked immensely relieved.

'I think that sounds grand.'

THE GIRL WHO TORE THROUGH THE UNIVERSE

NIKITA GILL

She is dreaming of the cliffs again. She is young here, a child. She's wearing a bright yellow summer dress and holding a woman's hand. The woman looks like her, so she assumes she is her mother. Everything is bright and happy here at the cliff edge. They are looking at an endless turquoise sea before them, glittering like jewels in the sunlight. But then she notices that her mother is not smiling. And, always too late, she sees the crack in the sky that looks just like the one in her wall. Before she can say a word, the crack opens like a mouth and devours her mother. She screams and tries to keep hold of her mother's hand . . .

And this was where Amy Pond usually woke up – unable to make sense of this strange, unsettling dream about a mother she didn't have . . . about a memory she was sure couldn't be real.

In a cold sweat, she reached for the glass of water by her bed, gulping at it. And then, as psychiatrist number three had taught her to do, she counted to ten. She had stopped trying to learn her psychiatrists' names. There was no point when they never lasted. And they never lasted because she kept biting them when they told her he wasn't real.

Her raggedy man.

Amy had been refusing to give up her raggedy man for eight years now. But she knew he was real because she remembered him too well. She remembered exactly how much he hated apples and loved fishfingers and custard. She remembered how quickly he was able to fix the crack in her wall. And, most of all, she remembered him saying he would come back for her. *Give me five minutes, I'll be right back,* he had told her before disappearing into the blue box. But the raggedy man hadn't come back. And a dozen adults including her aunt and school counsellor had told her that she was too old for imaginary friends. That the existence of her raggedy man was impossible and was all in her head.

Amy Pond may not know a lot of things yet, because she was only sixteen. But she knew that impossible things *could* happen. Men could fall out of boxes from the sky. A small blue police phone box could contain a swimming pool and library. And, most importantly, there was no reason why she couldn't do the impossible and bring her raggedy man back to show them all she was not making him up.

Her alarm rang loudly and she nearly jumped out of her skin. She smacked it silent and looked at the time. 7.15 a.m. She had to get ready for school.

School was her least favourite place in the world. Her teachers always said that Amy sat through classes constantly looking at the clock as though she had a train to catch. In essence, they were right. She did have somewhere else to be. Over the last eight years she had turned over every word her raggedy man had told her in her head until it made sense. 'Wibbly wobbly timey wimey' had something to do with physics, she was sure of it. So Amy had taken to going to the library during every lunch break, every free lesson, even in the ten minutes between fifth and sixth period, to learn everything she could about astronomy and physics, from Schrödinger to quantum theory.

She had yet to find anything to help her, but she always felt like she was so close. There was something she just couldn't see yet, something hiding in the corner of her eye . . . She walked into the school library, all white walls and cheap desks, a faint smell of mildew rising from carpets that had clearly seen thousands of wet student feet over the years and never been cleaned properly. As always, Amy made a beeline for the astronomy and physics section. It was a single bookcase with six shelves and Amy had read everything on the top four shelves. She crouched down to take a look at the bottom two. Mrs Mabel – the small, kind librarian with the cat glasses and the perpetually sniffly nose – had told her those shelves were for older students.

But Amy was already done with quantum theory for beginners. She was determined to devour everything she could so that one day, just one day, she could convince her aunt and those psychiatrists that her raggedy man was real.

Today she was reading Richard Feynman, and as she yanked the book out of its place, she saw two blue eyes staring back at her from behind a messy fringe.

Amy frowned and got up. She heard the person on the other side do the same and then a lanky boy put his head around the corner. 'Hello, sorry, I didn't mean to frighten you!'

Amy scoffed mildly. 'You didn't frighten me. It's a school library, there have to be other people here.'

The boy blushed beetroot red and scratched the back of his neck awkwardly. 'Sorry.'

Amy tilted her head. 'Do you always apologise so much?'

'Sor–' He blinked in confusion. 'I mean, yes, sometimes. I . . . er.'

Amy bit her lip to stop herself from laughing. 'Maybe I should apologise instead for scaring you, Rory?'

Rory Williams – tall, geeky – the quiet sort who kept himself out of trouble. They had been good friends until fairly recently, but had drifted apart in the last year. He smiled at her, his blush calming a little. Then she noticed the name of the book in his hand. *Scientific Mysteries, Oddities and Peculiarities.* Rory saw her interest and told her, 'I was supposed to be grabbing a book about computer programming for my IT class but got distracted by *this* on scientific mysteries instead.'

Amy grinned. 'Well, I like mysteries, and I like science.'

His eyes brightened and he looked at her own book. 'If you like quantum theories, I've actually got just the mystery for you.'

Without another word, they both sat down at the closest available desk and Rory opened the thick blue, gold-edged clothbound book that simply read *Scientific Mysteries, Oddities and Peculiarities* in embossing on the front. There was no author, Amy noted, but that wasn't important. After spending eight years in many, many libraries she knew that sometimes books survived past their authors and words lived long after their writers did.

Rory was flipping through the pages to the middle of the book, mumbling quietly to himself.

When he finally came to the page, he exclaimed, 'Hah! Found it!'

'Shhhhh!' came the loud stage whisper from the librarian's desk.

Rory grimaced and lowered his voice. 'OK, so here. Look at this. Did you know that when Isaac Newton died he left thousands of random papers and all sorts? They reckon if they put all his work together, it would produce, like, hundreds of books or something!'

Amy folded her arms and sat back, unconvinced. 'So? The man liked to write a lot. We all know that.'

Rory shook his head and pushed the book excitedly towards her. 'Yeah, but loads of his work went *missing*. All that stuff about alchemy just disappeared. It says here that just before he died, Newton talked about ripping through the fabric of space into the multiverse, that he could mess with time and –'

Before he could finish, Amy had grabbed the book and was looking through the pages, wide-eyed. 'Where? Show me where.'

Rory pointed out the passage to her and Amy read eagerly:

One of Newton's greatest tragedies, from which he never quite recovered, was the death of his father. He missed him terribly by all accounts and at a dinner party as a child announced that he was going to find a way to bring his father back. The adults at the table dismissed it as the whims and fancies of a child trying to understand death but, as time went on, Newton became even more determined. On three different occasions, servants at Woolsthorpe Manor saw Newton walking through a door to the dining room and seconds later coming out of his chambers. The dining room and chambers did not share any mutual doors. Nor did any secret rooms connect them. Each time the servants saw this odd behaviour, they claimed Newton was muttering, 'Almost managed that time, the formula needs more crafting.' More than that, servants reported doors where doors should not be and his housekeeper said one time the entire kitchen was swapped to a mirror image of itself. Of course there is no evidence to back up these claims but one has to wonder if Newton did ever manage to find a way into other universes. And if he did, where did the pages with those invaluable equations go?

Amy's hands were shaking by the time she got to the end of the paragraph. She put them on her knees so Rory wouldn't see.

'This is it,' she whispered, more to herself than him. 'The thing that lives in the corner of my eye.'

She looked up at Rory, who was watching her with his brow furrowed. 'Are you all right, Amy?'

'Yes. Yes, more than all right.' She smiled at him. 'Do you know where Woolsthorpe Manor is?'

Rory nodded. 'My mum took me there when I was younger. It's in Lincolnshire. It's really cool, actually. The National Trust made it into a museum and you can sit in the garden where the apple tree is . . .' He trailed off, seeing the glint in Amy's eye, and cleared his throat nervously. 'Why are you asking?'

She smiled sweetly and leaned forward. 'You wouldn't happen to know how to drive, would you, Rory Williams?'

It took them three hours to get to Lincolnshire in Rory's nan's old Fiat, but it felt more like three days. Amy was trying her best to be patient but it was hard. This was the closest she had ever come to something she was sure would bring her raggedy man back and every second felt like a quiet eternity.

But Rory was lovely. Amy had wondered briefly why Rory, who must have better things to do, was taking her all the way to Woolsthorpe Manor just because she asked. But perhaps he was looking for an adventure. And if there was one thing Amy Pond loved, it was adventure. They had both skipped a day of school. Rory had never ever done anything like this before – he was a straight-A student and had been extremely nervous as Amy put on a fake voice to sound like his mum on the phone. In the end she had sounded nothing like her, but they just about got away with it, and Amy had flicked her red hair back and laughed as they got into the rickety old car. 'I've done this tons of times. You need to live a little, Rory Williams.'

She could have asked her best friend, of course. But Mels was in huge trouble yet again for hiding all the costumes from the school's drama department before the play, and grounded – probably till she was thirty. Plus, she tended to get overexcited whenever the raggedy man was mentioned. Plus, there was absolutely no way Amy was getting anywhere near a car (even an old Fiat) if Mels Zucker was driving . . .

And so here they were. Going to Woolsthorpe Manor so that she could finally find what she was looking for and –

'So what are we doing at Woolsthorpe Manor, exactly?'

Amy came out of her daydream and looked at Rory, who was focusing hard on the road even though it was totally empty. She hesitated for a moment. 'We are going to . . . find

Isaac Newton's missing papers and find out . . . howtomakearipintime.'

The last part tumbled out so fast, she almost didn't realise she'd said it. But Rory had definitely heard it, because he whipped his head round to look at her. '*What?*'

Amy was about to say something when a deer pranced in front of them and Rory swerved off the country road to miss it. Amy cried out as the car jolted and Rory slammed on the brakes. They came to a shuddering stop at the side of the road. 'Sorry, are you OK?'

Rory's hands still clutched the steering wheel, and he was breathing fast as he looked at her.

She was breathing heavily too, her hands clenching the sides of the seat as she looked straight ahead, eyes wide, just like the deer on the road.

'Amy?' When she didn't turn to look at him, he repeated, 'Are you OK?'

She nodded ever so slightly. Then said, 'We need to find those papers.'

Rory sat back, releasing the steering wheel. He took a deep breath and said, 'OK. OK . . . Can you tell me why?'

'Nope.'

Amy's eyes were filling with tears but she blinked them away quickly. She knew that eventually she would have to tell him, but she didn't know how. Not without him thinking she was crazy, just like her psychiatrists and her aunt and the school counsellor. And she really didn't want to bite Rory when he was being so nice to her, and . . .

'Amy.' Rory reached out and put his hand gently on her clenched knuckles. 'It's all right. You don't need to tell me. I'll take you there. But you do know there's a big chance we won't find those notebooks, right? Plenty of people have probably tried. If they existed . . .' He chose his words carefully now. 'If they existed, they probably would have been found by now.'

Amy turned round to look at him, a quiet, fleeting vulnerability in her eyes. 'I have to try.' Then she swallowed hard. 'Please.'

He took a deep breath and silence flooded the car. Then he nodded. Her hands loosened as she saw him reach over to start the car up again, a part of her in disbelief that this boy would go out of his way to help her find something that he didn't believe existed. But the disbelief was quickly replaced with excitement and gratitude as he turned on to the road, looked at her and smiled reassuringly.

'Let's go find you those papers.'

Woolsthorpe Manor was smaller than she had expected but still beautiful. It was a stone house with rooms that looked as if they had been preserved in time. Everything seemed so *old*. It all came from a time when people could only write by hand, on parchment, with candlelight as a guide. And yet that was how Newton had changed the world –writing it all by hand.

Imagine what his missing papers could do.

Amy and Rory had spent most of their day searching this little space for those magical missing papers (and avoiding the prowling National Trust staff, who seemed determined to catch them out). But so far they had found absolutely nothing. Newton's bedroom contained a basic wooden bed, a small, ornate wooden desk and an equally carefully crafted wooden stool. The bed had deliberately been arranged to look like Newton had just got out of it, and pieces of paper with scribbles and equations were strewn about the place.

Amy first checked under the bed while Rory nervously kept watch. Luckily for them, there weren't a lot of people here at three in the afternoon on a Wednesday. But there was nothing but dust. She stood up and frowned. Then she ran her hands along the carvings of the desk. A secret drawer perhaps? Maybe a catch somewhere?

She was disappointed once again to find nothing.

Then she looked at the walls. Perhaps there was something there? She got up and ran her hands over them,

seeking a loose brick she may have missed, but if there was
one she couldn't find it. Rory was now shifting from one leg to
the other, watching her then looking back to make sure no
one was walking in. 'Hurry up, Amy.'

She glared at him over her shoulder. 'I'm trying!' She
pushed against the stones of the wall, then stood back
reluctantly.

'Nothing here,' she sighed.

Rory looked like he was going to say something but
before he could she growled, 'Don't say *I told you so.*'

'I wasn't!' he said defensively, but the look on his face
told her different.

Together they walked downstairs and into the garden,
Amy deep in thought and Rory glancing at her every now
and then, trying to think of what to say to make it better. As
they wandered through the garden, Rory pointed out, 'Look,
that's the apple tree!'

There it was. The tree that Newton had sat under while
crafting his equations, where he had discovered the theory of
gravity as he watched the apples fall in a straight line to the
ground. His most famous theory. So important was this tree
to Newton's work that it had been celebrated on the golden
jubilee of Queen Elizabeth, as an essential part of English
history. It was encircled by a fence which did more to show

the importance of the tall, beautiful tree than to offer any actual protection. The tree hadn't yet started producing fruit, it was too early in the season, but the sweet smell of its flowers filled the air.

Apples had always reminded Amy of her family, somehow. She had a strange memory of smiley faces carved into the skin, to encourage her to eat them . . .

Amy stared at the tree for a long time, an idea unfurling itself inside her head. Her eyes brightened suddenly. 'Rory, you're a genius.'

Surprised, Rory turned to her. But Amy had already stepped over the fence and moved behind the tree. She started digging into the soft, wet earth around the tree with her hands.

'Amy, what are you –'

'Where would you hide notebooks if you had discovered the secrets to the universe? You'd keep them in a place that you considered sacred, right? Where else would you put something that meant so much to you?' She dug and dug until her fingers hit a small rusted tin box. A massive smile spread across her face as she began to dig faster, her fingers catching on a root every now and then. Finally, she put both her hands round the box and yanked hard. It didn't budge the first time she yanked. But the second time it came loose and sent Amy flying, landing on her back. Rory rushed over to help her up.

Then a loud voice from the manor yelled, 'Oi, you two! What do you think you're doing?!'

Amy and Rory looked up to see a tall man in glasses and a brown suit running over to them, his face red with fury.

The curator!

Without another word, Amy clutched the box to her chest, Rory grabbed her free hand and they ran.

They were sitting in Rory's car now. It took a lot of effort with Rory's penknife to fiddle the lock on the tin box open. Amy waited impatiently, trying to get the dirt out from under her fingernails. Finally, after what felt like hours but was probably only minutes, Rory managed it.

The box creaked painfully as its lid fell open and Amy immediately dug her hand in to draw out several yellowed pieces of parchment.

Equations they couldn't decipher spread across the sheets, drawn in ink and pencil. A sketch of a door. A sketch of a knife. Several geometric designs. But finally Amy saw the words she was looking for.

Doorways to Other Universes.

Amy knew how the multiverse worked. She knew there was another Amy Pond in a different universe who got to travel with her raggedy man, just as he had promised her. And she thought that if she made a deep enough rip in the fabric of this universe, her raggedy man might be on the other side.

She turned to look at Rory, a massive smile on her face, and tossed her arms around him, the papers clutched in her hands.

He hugged her back, blushing deeply. He had found the most beautiful, brave girl in the world and she had already achieved the impossible in twenty-four hours.

It almost didn't matter when his eyes fell on a piece of parchment that had fallen out of the tin, now lying on the floor by Amy's foot. It almost didn't worry him that a warning was written on it in ancient black ink:

'*Be wary. For here lies the unspeakable.*'

Three weeks. It had been three long, frustrating weeks since they had opened the tin and found the equations. They had tried everything, even surreptitiously asking their physics teacher for help. But that had proved useless. Mr Brown had just got suspicious and asked them so many questions Rory turned bright red and Amy had to grab his arm and drag him out of the room, making a dozen excuses.

The equations might as well have been an ancient spell in a forgotten tongue. No amount of imagination, mathematical training or physics lessons seemed to be working and Amy had burst into tears enough times to be close to giving up . . .

. . . until last night. The instructions – written in tiny writing below the mass of equations – had seemed much too straightforward. Amy knew it couldn't be that simple, which was why she had refused to even entertain the idea of trying this method before. How could it possibly be that simple when the rest of Newton's notes were so complex?

But then, last night, Amy had stood outside her bedroom, door closed, and decided to try. She closed her eyes and pictured her raggedy man. He was standing there with his screwdriver, fixing the crack in her wall. She could see herself tossing him an apple. See him asking her why there was a smiley face on it and hear her answer: 'My mum used to make those for me.' She saw him so clearly, as though the memory was from yesterday. How he put the apple in her pocket and said, 'She sounds good, your mum.' But then in a moment the memory was gone, as if it had never been there . . .

THUNK.

Amy's eyes opened wide. Her fingers trembled. She raised her hand to the brass handle of her bedroom door.

Light poured through from the gaps around the edges, as though something very bright was hiding behind.

Pleasepleaseplease.

Slowly, she pushed the door open. The light was so bright that for a minute she felt blinded. When it subsided, she blinked slowly. A familiar kitchen came into view. And there she was. The woman from her dream. Her mother. Putting an apple pie on the old wooden kitchen table which looked like it was going to collapse any second. Her favourite green jumper and jeans on, red hair swept back in a messy bun, the same flowery apron Amy couldn't believe she had forgotten. For a moment, she was stunned as she watched her mother hum and pull out the custard from the fridge, just as she had pictured in her head. How had she forgotten this? Her home in Leadworth, her mother's face, the kitchen table. It was like a flood of memories escaped into her mind from behind a door within her head. She'd tried to find her raggedy man, but instead she'd discovered a person she never knew she'd lost.

Her mum turned round and noticed her. She didn't even look surprised as she said, 'Oh good, you're back.' Her mother set the custard on the table. 'I know apple pie isn't your favourite. But I promised your father we'd have it for tea today and –'

She was cut off by the huge hug she found herself wrapped in. Startled, mum wrapped her arms round Amy. 'Amelia? Are you all right, my love?'

Amy pulled back and looked into her mother's surprised eyes. They were the exact same shade as her own.

But . . . how? How had she ended up here? Amy went through the notes in her mind. She had followed them precisely. The thing she desired most was what she pictured, and *the thing she desired most held one of the only memories she had of her mother*. Shaking her head clear of racing thoughts, a sense of urgency overcame her. She knew she couldn't let her mother see that urgency, else she would clock that something was wrong. Newton's notes were quite clear that if you did encounter someone from another universe, you needed to make sure they didn't catch on. He never explained *what* would happen if they did; he'd just written an ominous warning that you shouldn't let them become aware. But that wasn't a good enough reason for Amy to leave her mother so soon after finding her. She might never find her again. 'Mum, you need to come with me.' She took her mother's hand urgently, trying to literally drag her to the door.

'Amelia . . . Amelia!' Her mother pulled her hand away. 'We can't go anywhere. Your father will be home any minute and –'

Amy was visibly shaking now. She wanted to wait for her dad and bring him home too. But she couldn't risk staying here too long. She didn't know how much time they had. She hadn't studied the notes to know how long she could make the portal work. 'Mum, please. I'll explain when I show you, OK?'

A long, agonising pause followed and her mother sighed. She took off her flowery apron and said, 'I hope this is important, Amelia.'

Amy visibly relaxed as she replied, 'I promise you, Mum, it's a matter of life and death.'

Things had gone wrong. Horribly wrong. The minute her mother stepped through the doorway, her chatty, normal self had vanished and she had sunk into a zombie-like state. Now she simply stared straight ahead of her, like a person in shock. Behind them, the portal had closed as quickly as it had opened and in place of the kitchen was Amy's bedroom. Hours had passed like this, with no sign of her mother speaking or communicating. Amy had sat her at the kitchen table in her aunt's house. She had tried everything. She had tried talking to her and cajoling her, telling her how much she loved her, even placing an apple and a small butterknife on the table, to make her carve the apple like Amy remembered. And then when all else failed, in frustration, she had screamed at her.

Nothing got a reaction. Her mother continued to stare blankly ahead, a shell of the woman she was just hours ago.

Her aunt would know what to do. But Amy's aunt was on another business trip. She went away often enough that Amy was used to being alone. But, right now, she needed someone else, anyone, here to help her. The raggedy man would definitely know what to do; he would probably have something in his box that could help . . .

She almost jumped out of her skin as Rory burst in through the kitchen door.

'Have you seen the sky –' His excitement died as soon as he saw the woman sitting at the table. 'Amy . . .' he said slowly, 'who is this?'

'My . . . my mum.' And after saying that Amy burst into tears. Immediately, Rory was by her side, crouching and putting his arms round her.

'She just sits there,' sobbed Amy. 'She won't move or do anything. She just sits there quietly like . . . like she's in shock. Newton was right, I should have never brought her back here –'

Rory pulled back as she said this. 'You did it? You made the portal?'

Rory looked to the woman again, the wide-eyed, unblinking stare making him wince with discomfort. He waved a hand in front of her face to try to make her blink.

Nothing. He swallowed hard as he turned to gaze out of the kitchen window in contemplation, joining the dots in his mind. 'I think there's something you need to see.' He pointed at the sky through the kitchen window.

When Amy Pond saw what was outside, her first reaction wasn't an exclamation or a question. Instead, she looked at the kitchen clock to check what time it was.

Nope. Eight o clock in the morning didn't explain it.

She couldn't ever remember seeing neon-green sky and birds that flew upside down.

'What . . . what is happening?' she asked no one in particular, her voice small and afraid. Rory had never once heard Amy afraid. And now he knew that he hated to hear Amy Pond afraid even more than he hated to hear her sad. Because there were not many things that Rory Williams believed in. But he believed in Amy Pond's confidence and courage more than anything in the world.

Quietly, he reached out to take her hand as they looked at the chaos slowly unfolding before them, feeling like the last people in the world.

The hundred-year-old trees in the garden were starting to age before their eyes, leaves turning black and blue like bruises as they hit the ground. The grass, usually dewy at this time of the morning, seemed to be ageing backwards, becoming a series of sprouts before disappearing into the ground. But the worst were the flowers. The flowers simply caught fire.

And, through all this, Amy's mother sat still, unmoving, unblinking.

Not knowing what to do, Amy slumped down at the table in a heap. Rory sat on the chair between Amy and her mum, his face in his hands.

Outside, things kept changing rapidly. The world looked like it was both beginning and ending at once.

Finally, Rory said it. His voice shook as he spoke a terrible truth he had been keeping secret all this time.

'I think we've made a huge mistake, Amy. I think those pages were buried for a reason. I think Isaac Newton left us that warning for a reason. These are the unspeakable things that he was talking about. We should never have done this.'

Amy looked at him, her hazel eyes wide. 'Are you saying this is my fault?'

And for the first time, instead of denying it to protect her feelings, Rory was quiet.

Because she was right. She was the reason this was happening. But even though she had wrecked the fabric of the universe, Rory couldn't bear to see Amy sad. So instead, he looked into her dejected eyes. 'You can fix this. If anyone can fix it, it's you.'

Amy shook her head. 'I don't even know where to begin!'

'You're Amy Pond – the girl who found Newton's missing papers and ripped a hole in the fabric of the universe. You can do this, Amy. I promise.' Confidence glinted in Rory's eyes – a confidence Amy desperately needed to share.

But tears were streaking down her face again, and she shook her head. 'I don't understand what you're saying.'

As gently as he could, Rory reached out and took Amy's cold hand in both of his warm ones. When she finally looked at his face, his voice was soft. 'Yes, Amy. You do.' He looked at the woman across the table. 'You know exactly what you need to do.'

Amy took a deep, shuddering breath and slowly stood up. Gently, Rory let Amy's hand go and went to stand beside her mother's chair.

After a few minutes, Amy wiped her face and sighed. 'Let's do this.'

The fact that it had worked the first time was incredible. Making it work again was a near-impossible task. But Amy was brave and determined.

And she was devastated.

Perhaps there was a kind, old force within the universe which took pity on her. This time when she pictured the old kitchen that she had been in just hours ago – smelling the apple pie and the custard, picturing herself, a girl with two parents who loved her and a mother who still carved smiley faces in apples – it worked.

She opened the door quietly just in time to see her father walk through the kitchen door, whistling as he went into the living room to find his family. As soon as she knew the coast was clear, she gestured to Rory and together they helped her mother towards the door. It was a good thing that, though she wasn't speaking, she could still walk.

Amy smiled at Rory and nodded, letting him know she could take it from here.

He stood back as Amy and her mother crossed the threshold, keeping a watchful eye on both of them.

As soon as she was in her kitchen, Amy's mother woke from her unblinking trance like she had emerged from a daze.

She looked at her daughter in surprise and said, 'I thought you were taking me somewhere.'

Amy had always thought that growing up without parents was the most painful thing she would ever have to do. She was wrong. Losing her mother a second time was so much worse than the first because she could barely remember the first. This . . . this felt like every single part of her heart was crushed again after she had put it back together so painstakingly. But right now her mother was smiling a worried smile, and raising her hand to Amy's forehead to check if she was all right.

Amy took a step back. 'I'll be OK, Mum.'

Her mother frowned slightly. 'Are you sure?'

Amy took a deep, shaky breath. 'I'll be OK.' She took one last long look at her mother, and tried to burn the image of her into her memory so that she could cherish this forever. 'I promise I'll be OK.'

And with those words Amy Pond gave her mother one final hug and walked through the door that had brought her here, closing it behind her with a soft click.

Amy stood outside the door a long, long time. She could already feel the memories of her mother fading again, no matter how hard she tried to hold on to them. Tears ran freely down her face when she finally let go of the handle and walked into the kitchen to get some water.

As she entered, she saw the apple on the table and nearly broke down in sobs. Walking over to it, she lifted it in her hand.

A smiley face had been carved into the apple.

She smiled. This must have been Rory's doing. Trying to make her feel better.

Amy searched the house for him. Just when she decided he must have gone home, she found him sitting on the roof. She would have asked why he was out there but the question seemed like a silly one considering everything else that had happened.

So instead she climbed out of her bedroom window and sat next to him. He smiled and gestured to the horizon.

Amy looked out to see that the sky was very slowly turning from the bright neon-green to the azure she had known her whole life. Below, she could see the trees were alive again and the grass was no longer just seeds within the ground. The flowers in the garden were as bright and vibrant as they always had been.

Amy breathed out a sigh of relief and closed her eyes as she felt a comfortable tiredness. She felt Rory take her hand.

'Thank you for the apple,' she said softly.

'What apple?' he asked.

She pulled it out of her jacket pocket and showed him. 'This one.'

Rory took the apple and stared at it. 'What about it?'

Amy lifted her head. 'You carved it for me.'

The confused look on Rory's face told Amy everything she needed to know.

She took the apple back from Rory and quietly placed it in her pocket. Then, with a sigh, she leaned her head against his shoulder.

Together they peacefully watched the sky become blue again.

And while everything wasn't all right, for the first time in her life Amy Pond truly believed that it would be. One day.

CLARA OSWALD AND THE ENCHANTED FOREST

JASBINDER BILAN

Morning sunshine burst through the window as Clara grabbed her phone from the bedside table. Things had been tough lately. She couldn't do a thing right as far as her mum was concerned – they'd been rowing about the tiniest little detail.

She tapped out a reply to her best friend, Ashari.

Need to persuade Mum to let me sleep over. Shouldn't be hard!!

Clara couldn't wait for this Halloween party. Not *just* because Ashari had persuaded Gem to come, but he *was* just the loveliest, most thoughtful boy in Year Ten. And pretty cool too – he had dark hair which he wore swept off his beautiful golden face.

Clara looked at herself in the mirror and blew her brown fringe off her own face.

'Hi, Gem,' she practised. 'Fancy seeing you here!'

They had a few classes together but they didn't know each other too well. But what Clara *did* know was that every time she saw him, her legs turned to jelly. The party would be a chance for them to hang out together.

Clara's phone pinged with another message from Ashari.

Bring your party clothes to mine for 7. Mum's going to drive us.

'Clara!' her mum called up the stairs. 'You've left the kitchen in a right mess from last night.'

Clara went out on to the landing. 'Keep your hair on, Mum. It's not that bad.'

'Get down here now.'

Here we go again. Clara sidled down the stairs.

'Don't talk to me like that,' warned her mum, walking back into the kitchen. She sat down at the table and began reading through some work notes. She glanced at Clara, who was still standing in the doorway.

'Sorry.' Clara didn't mean to annoy her mum, today of all days. She was meant to be persuading her to let her sleep over at Ashari's tonight. 'I'll do it now,' she said, as she began loading the dishwasher.

'Mum?'

'Yes?' She carried on reading her notes.

'You know this party I'm going to tonight?'

She looked up, a frown grazing her forehead. 'I didn't know you were going to a party.'

Clara felt her cheeks turn hot. 'I told you last week. It's a Halloween party . . . and *everyone's* sleeping over.'

'Well, not you.'

'You never let me do anything. *Please*. I'm nearly fifteen.'

'I've said no – it's final, Clara. I don't want you sleeping over, especially on Halloween. People do all sorts of things on nights like that.'

'What sorts of things? Like some bloodsucking vampire digging his teeth into my neck?' Clara's words dripped with sarcasm.

'You can go for a couple of hours and your dad'll pick you up, before things get silly.'

'Mum, please!' Hot tears stung Clara's cheeks.

'I'm sorry, Clara, it's for the best.'

Clara slammed the kitchen door and thumped up the stairs to her bedroom. She wanted to show her mum just how upset she was. Picking up her book, the one her mum had read to her every night when she was little, Clara opened the window.

Her mum thundered up the stairs after her and stood in the doorway. 'I'm not changing my mind – it's final.'

Clara held the book in front of her mum and turned the pages until she found the leaf that had brought her parents together all those years ago. It might seem silly, but this leaf was the most important thing to Clara's family – and to Clara.

She picked it out of the book and held it in her trembling hands and, as her mum's eyes widened in shock, Clara let the precious thing fly out of the open window into the air.

They both watched as the wind caught the leaf, lifted it into the sky and blew it away.

'Clara!' It was her mum's turn to cry now. 'Clara, how could you?' Her mum ran down the stairs, opened the kitchen door and stared into the sky, but the treasured leaf had vanished.

Clara stuffed her party gear into a bag and slammed out of the house.

*

After school had finished Clara and Ashari picked up some chips, then headed over to Ashari's house. But in the back of her mind Clara knew that throwing the leaf out of the window had been a step too far . . . and it was too late now.

She pushed the sad feelings away and thought about Gem instead. 'He's definitely coming, isn't he?' she asked.

'I told him he had to, otherwise he'd have me to answer to.' Ashari laughed, pushing her fingers through her short purple-tipped hair. She slotted her key into the front door and shoved it open. 'Quick, let's get upstairs before Dad starts on at us.'

'Is that you, Ashari?'

She popped her head into the sitting room. 'Yeah, Dad – Clara's here. We're going to get ready for Satchen's party.'

Clara followed Ashari to her bedroom. They put on music and started to get ready. Clara pulled out her crumpled dress from the rucksack. She was going for a gothic vampire look, so the creases added to her character.

Clara wriggled into the black, sparkly dress and holey tights and pushed her feet into red Doc Martens.

Ashari whistled. 'Here, let me do your make-up.' She carefully loaded blood-red lipstick on to Clara's lips and went heavy with the black eyeliner.

'I'm going for vampire beauty,' said Clara, 'not Cruella de Vil. Make it look cool!'

Ashari's mum drove them to the gates of the party. The house was at the far edge of town where the verges were wide and leafy and the houses had vast, rambling gardens. It was dark already and the yellow moon poked out through the shadow-shimmer of the clouds.

'Are you sure you'll be OK?' asked Ashari's mum. 'I can take you right in if you like.'

'No, Mum.' Ashari rolled her eyes. 'Here's fine!'

Clara glanced at her phone.

Clara – let me know where you are. I love you Mum X

Her finger hovered over the text but, instead of replying, Clara ignored her mum's message and shoved the phone away.

As Clara and Ashari made their way down the winding driveway, the house – strung with ghoulish bat lights – glowed ahead of them. Clara felt a sudden shiver prickle along her spine and imagined shadows hiding between the darkened branches. When they arrived at the front door a pumpkin screamed silently at them with its menacing mouth.

They followed a *PARTY* sign gripped in a skeletal hand round to a brick barn deeper inside the garden. Clara knocked on the door and music thumped out into the night as the door opened and they were swallowed into the belly of the party.

It was heaving inside the barn. Clara and Ashari pushed their way through the dancing bodies, dressed in all sorts of costumes, and grabbed themselves Cokes from the table laden with scary-faced mini pizzas, sausage rolls and bowls of crisps.

'Look, there's Gem.' Ashari caught hold of Clara's hand and dragged her across to him.

He was dressed as a vampire too, with white, dusty make-up and a line of blood dripping from his lips. His hair was gelled back, except for the strand that flopped over his eyes – as usual.

'Hello,' said Clara shyly.

'Hi,' replied Gem, clearing his throat.

The three of them danced together, taking breaks for food and drink until someone suggested a game of hide-and-seek in the woods at the back of the house.

'Come on!' a voice cried. 'If you're brave enough.'

'It's really dark out there,' said Clara.

'You're not scared, are you?' laughed Gem. 'What could happen?'

'He's right,' agreed Ashari. 'The woods aren't big, only a few trees, really.'

Before she could think any more about it, Clara was being led out of the barn into the darkness.

The forest – to Clara it was more of a forest than a wood – was filled with shifting shadows. Huge branches towered over them, high-pitched chattering sounds echoing to and fro. Clara could still see the house from here, the hazy lights twinkling in the near distance.

'Right, let's play!' someone cried, their voice faint among the crowded trees. 'You're it, Clara.'

'Will you be OK by yourself?' asked Ashari.

'Course,' replied Clara, trying to sound braver than she felt.

'Sure?'

Clara was already scared – she hated being alone – but she couldn't lose face, especially not in front of Gem. 'Yeah, go. I'm counting.'

Gem and Ashari ran to join the dancing group from the barn, their laughter mingling with the low hoots of owls. And another strange sound – the cracking of tree roots.

Clara finished counting to a hundred and opened her eyes. The lonely thrum of her heartbeat pounded in her ears as she swallowed and peered through the thick, dark forest.

The trees loomed around Clara, closing in, their gnarled roots ready to trip her up. Shapes flitted around the forest floor and dreamlike sounds spun their way to her as she tried to push down the fear.

She thought she heard shouts and raced off in their direction until she was in the middle of a clearing, the bright moon beating down on her. But there was nobody here.

She let out a small cry. 'Where's the house?'

Shivers bumped up her spine – all the trees looked the same. The awful truth thumped at her belly. She was already lost.

A sudden memory of the time she got lost on Blackpool beach brought tears to her eyes. But her mum had found her. Mum had said she'd always find her, even if she was on the moon. She'd made Clara feel so safe. Clara remembered the touch of her palm against her mum's and suddenly wished her mum was here now. She'd know exactly what to do.

Clara wiped her cheek on her sleeve and told herself to grow up. Her mum was back at home, and anyway . . . Clara didn't know if she'd ever forgive her for losing the precious leaf.

She stared out towards the trees again, their ridged bark running up the trunks in furrows, their gangly branches sharp against the moonlight. A strange cracking sound froze Clara to the spot. They were moving!

She forced herself to stop being melodramatic. Trees didn't move. She blinked, then rubbed her eyes, but she was convinced now that the trees really were creeping towards her. As they got closer, she saw sneering faces on the bark, and her chest tightened.

With each crack of their roots they moved towards Clara. Should she make a run for it, ducking under their branches?

What if they caught her?

Blood pumped fast round her body and she made tight fists, trying to calm herself. But each moment she did nothing, the trees were crowding in. Clara felt a long spiky arm grab hold of her and roots tangle round her legs. She felt paralysed!

She screamed and made a grab for the lower branches of the closest tree, the only one that wasn't moving and wasn't part of this terrifying herd surrounding her.

Clara tried to climb up. Just above her head she saw a hollow in the tree, lit up by moonlight, and slotted her hand in. Using all her strength, she thrashed and wriggled herself free of the grappling, grasping roots of the moving trees.

But they came for her again with their writhing tentacles and tried to trap her once more, whipping their roots along the length of the trunk, using them like ropes to haul themselves up.

Panting for breath, she stretched up, desperate to get away, and continued to climb towards the moon, diving between the upper branches. But the cracking below was louder and more furious with each step Clara took. She didn't dare look back, and stared ahead instead, her arms trembling as she hoisted herself higher and higher. As if she was climbing up to the stars.

She gasped.

Before her, suspended in the sky, was a blue box, a bit like a phone box but wooden and with a light on top. It was just . . . there, above the forest, in a wave of shimmering white mist. The door was flung open and yellow light shone out from it. *What was this?*

Balancing at the very top of the tree, Clara felt a crooked branch grab for her. It grazed her foot and she screamed. *What should she* do? A tendril began to snake around her ankle.

Clara sensed curious eyes watching her from above, through the canopy of autumn leaves. The blue box seemed to manoeuvre closer, as if it was shifting to help Clara escape the trees.

She shook off the branch and leaped into the open box, gripping the door frame. Trembling, she hauled herself away from the trees and into the unknown.

'Who are you?' Clara asked in disbelief, staring at a rather startled-looking man in a fancy red bow tie and tweed jacket. She swallowed.

'Oh! Erm . . . hello! I'm the Doctor.'

Her mum had always told her not to speak to strange men, and yet here she was. She couldn't help herself, though, it was as if she'd met him before. His big smile and wide eyes seemed so familiar . . . 'Doctor *Who*?'

'Correct – now come in if you're coming,' he said, adjusting his bow tie. 'I'm in the middle of something very clever and fiddly.' He began to poke at a few buttons on an old-fashioned typewriter which made up part of the elaborate controls in front of him and the door closed.

'I was being chased by t-trees.' Clara felt a little silly now.

'Ah yes! Nasty, grabby trees. Big nuisance!' He stared into the controls and his face lit up. 'I *think* those trees might be dormant life forms from another planet.'

Clara put her hand over her mouth to stop the giggles. 'Do you mean aliens?!' she said, laughing. Suddenly all the fear from earlier flew away.

'I'm glad you've cheered up and, yes, aliens, I suppose. I've an idea they were feeding off you somehow. Off your . . . uncertainty.' He looked closely at Clara.

'Mmm.' She took a step back from him and stared around, for the first time properly taking in the room. She felt a sudden tug of nerves. 'But the police box – it looked so small on the outside. How can it be so incredible on the inside?'

The man laughed. 'Magic!' He waved his hands mysteriously. 'Not really. Just a nifty bit of science with a big dollop of imagination. Welcome to the TARDIS. Now, where do you want to go? Actually, no, first things first. What's your name?' He looked directly at her again.

Clara reddened. She hesitated, then held out her hand to the Doctor. 'It's Clara, Clara Oswald. Pleased to meet you.'

He crinkled his brow, thinking. 'Clara Oswald? Er – no, I mean, not meant to happen now. Got my dates muddled, just wanted to check on you. Should've known it would backfire.'

Clara felt her heart thump. 'You're not making any sense.'

'Sorry. Forget all of that. Pleased to meet you, Clara Oswald the – er – vampire!'

Clara had forgotten about her outfit and she blushed again. The evening was getting weirder by the minute.

Suddenly, the phone box lurched to one side. Clara managed to glimpse out of the window as she was thrown towards the doors. Her friends were still down there, calling out to her. The forest was alive around them. The trees were staring up with menacing eyes, clawing at the sky. But it was as though her friends couldn't see the trees – like the only person they wanted was Clara.

Then the phone box lurched again, and the cracking sound of roots being sucked out of the earth became fainter and fainter.

'We're flying away! Take me back!' she shouted, fear gripping her again. 'Please take me back to my friends.'

'I'm doing my best,' said the Doctor, yanking at various controls in a flurry of motion. 'But the TARDIS doesn't always do what she's told.' He grinned at her.

The TARDIS suddenly began to spin wildly, flinging both Clara and the Doctor against the walls. They whirred through the sky as Clara scrambled back to the window, panic gripping her chest. Outside, stars spun past her at flicker-speed and Clara felt like she was drifting further away from everything she knew. She closed her eyes and tried to stop her stomach from turning somersaults.

After what seemed like an eternity but was really only seconds, they finally came to a shuddering stop. They had landed back in the forest.

The door opened and Clara ran out. 'Oh my stars! We're back – and the trees are normal again,' she cried.

The air was fresh and filled with the rich scents of ancient woodland: leaves trodden underfoot, fresh shoots and apple blossom.

Clara couldn't see her friends anywhere. But that didn't matter – she was back. She continued towards the moss-coated trees with leaves as wide as palms.

'Clara!' called the Doctor. 'Come back. I think I might have got my landing a bit off. It's not the same forest!'

But Clara didn't hear. She was caught in the spell of this place. Above her a halo of stars shot against the indigo night and the bright silver moon hung like a delicate fingernail in the sky. In the far-off distance the peaks of snow-capped mountains rose as tall as giants.

It was like she was always meant to find this place. She knew this wasn't where she'd left Gem and Ashari, but there was something so familiar and safe about it. She didn't feel frightened, but stepped with wonder through the moon-dappled trees. They were the complete opposite of the ones in the other forest: they welcomed her with warm and loving energy, as if she belonged.

She spotted a shadow ahead and, without quite knowing why, hurried forward, trying to catch up with it.

'Clara, wait!' she heard the Doctor calling behind her. 'I can't keep up! Tweed jackets and pointy branches don't combine well . . . Argh, I'm stuck!' But Clara was already too enchanted to listen.

The white wolf sat waiting for Clara. Its fur, silky and fine, its ears alert, listening to the forest hum. It was tucked into the shadow of a grand tree and when it saw Clara it blinked deep-hazel eyes rimmed green and leaf brown.

Clara paused, fear suddenly shooting through her. But the wolf sat still and fixed her again with its eyes like autumn leaves. She felt a familiar tug at her heart and sprinted towards the wolf, throwing her arms round the white body. This was a mother wolf, Clara somehow knew, and she felt her gentle heartbeat against her own. It made no sense, but it was as if they had known each other Clara's whole life.

Rising up, the she-wolf led Clara further into the forest, and together they disappeared into this new world.

*

The wolf showed Clara a huge hollow tree beside a fast-flowing river . . . just as the first flakes of winter snow began to fall.

The wolf padded across to the hollow and rested on a thick bed of fallen leaves. Clara joined her and placed her head against the comfort of the she-wolf's fur. A memory from long ago wended its way to Clara; she remembered being wrapped safely in a blanket beside her mum, and Mum's voice telling Clara that she would always protect her, no matter what.

An unexpected tear froze on Clara's cheek and then the memory, like a precious diamond, tinkled to the ground.

When Clara looked into the sky, the moon appeared again from between the clouds, lighting up a scooped-out hole in the gnarled branch above her head. She stood on tiptoe and pressed her fingers into the hole. There she found something, something worn smooth by loving hands.

'It's the leaf!' she cried, unbelieving. 'Mum and Dad's leaf.'

She couldn't explain it. She couldn't explain any of this. But she'd found the leaf again, and that was a miracle. Once she got home she'd make it up to her mum. She knew this with certainty, though she couldn't explain why. Clara tucked the leaf safely in her pocket and turned to face the she-wolf again.

She was bent over the water that ran smooth and river-green past the hollow tree. It was still snowing and everything was painted an ethereal white.

Clara went to join the she-wolf at the river's edge and together they stared into the water – into their past lives and their future ones.

Looking into the river as it swept across the stones, Clara sensed something else. The Doctor, somehow, in her future. But the thought drifted away under the icy water on its way to a distant sea.

None of it mattered. She let her body fill with a happiness that she'd never really felt before. She knew that whatever happened everything would be OK. She'd return the leaf and make everything right with her mum.

The she-wolf nudged Clara's hand open and on the sloping banks of the river she dropped something into Clara's outstretched palm.

Clara stared at the piece of bright amber lit by moonlight. It was incredible. Perfectly preserved inside was the most delicate feather.

She was so enthralled with the amber that she didn't see her she-wolf leave, but when she lifted her head to the hollow tree it was empty. She felt her heart patter. A fierce howl echoed through the forest and the word *trust* sprang into Clara's mind.

Her she-wolf must have been as silent as a shadow. Clara saw fresh paw prints marking the snow and hurried to follow. She heard the howl again and ahead of her she saw the she-wolf, raised on her hind legs, facing a snarling sabre-toothed tiger.

The tiger was bigger than the she-wolf, with bronze, mottled fur and two immense dripping canines. It towered above the smaller creature.

Fear snapped at Clara as the tiger pounced at the wolf, batting her to the ground with its powerful paw. The tiger suddenly turned as it spotted Clara, and made to attack. But the she-wolf was between them in a heart beat. She grew fiercer, her eyes full of fire as she leaped at the sabretooth.

Clara took out the leaf from her pocket and with shaking hands held it up to the incredible tiger. If the leaf had brought her parents together, maybe it really did have magical powers. The sabretooth shrank back, turned and miraculously retreated towards the mountains.

'Oh my stars!' she murmured, her heart fluttering like a trapped butterfly. She put the leaf back in her pocket.

The she-wolf led Clara back to the hollow tree and they rested by the river until a yellow haze filled the whole forest. In the near distance, she saw a shape fading in and out of existence, lit golden by the glow. A wheezing, grinding noise floated across the glade.

Something was arriving. Clara had to shield her eyes as a blue brightness shone out of the object like a thousand suns.

'It's that box again,' said Clara. 'And the Doctor.'

The spell was broken. Clara buried her head in the she-wolf's fur. 'Until the next time,' she whispered.

The strange Doctor man who had brought her here was waiting in the entrance of the open TARDIS. He was smiling softly. 'I won't ask what happened here, if you don't want to tell me,' he said very gently. 'But I have got the TARDIS working again. Want a lift?'

This was amazing! Clara held out her hand and felt a spark pass through it as the Doctor hauled her back inside the glowing TARDIS.

'I'm glad I found you again,' he said, a twinkle in his eye. 'I thought I'd lost you.'

'I had an adventure,' said Clara. 'It was strange but . . . wonderful.'

'And I found this.' Clara fished the autumn leaf from deep inside her pocket. 'It's very special. You won't believe me but it's the exact same leaf that brought my parents together.'

'You'd be surprised by the things I believe, Clara Oswald.'

'I'm so glad I found it. I had a row with Mum this morning and threw it out of the window.'

The Doctor looked sad, suddenly. He straightened his bow tie and cleared his throat. 'Well, that sounds like *quite* a leaf. Keep it safe from now on. You never know when it might come in handy.'

'Definitely.' Clara put the leaf back in her pocket. 'And I met a she-wolf. She gave me this.' She held out the bright piece of amber. 'I think it's maybe thousands of years old.'

'Let me see.' The Doctor examined it with a magnifying glass he'd produced from the inside pocket of his tweed jacket. 'Correction – millions of years old.'

'OK, clever clogs, what sort of bird is the feather from?'

'Not a bird.' He tapped his head. 'A dinosaur!'

'What!' cried Clara, looking over the Doctor's shoulder.

'*This* dinosaur would have lived millions of years ago, a long time before you, Clara. It was the size of a small bird. The feather probably got trapped in the tree resin while it was searching for grubs.'

This ancient piece of tree resin that had survived millions of years. Maybe the she-wolf just thought it was a beautiful object. But maybe, just maybe, she was trying to give Clara an important message. That some things are fleeting, but some leave their mark forever. Ancient and indestructible. It was a reminder of the infinity of life.

'OK.' Clara smiled. 'Can I have it back now? I'm going to have it made into a necklace.'

'Good idea! Don't get too attached to it, though – you might lose it.'

'I won't lose it.'

'Just saying – you might. You never know. And anyway, it's OK, we have to let some things go.'

Clara frowned.

'Where shall we go, then?' the Doctor asked quickly, before pushing his hands through his floppy hair like he suddenly regretted asking the question.

He returned to the panel of switches and busied himself, turning them on and off.

In a daze, Clara leaned against the wall. 'Is there a kitchen in here? I'd love a cup of tea.'

'Of course! Can't have a spaceship without a kitchen. Mine's milk and two sugars, please.' He looked at her again with that searching gaze.

'I want to go home,' Clara finally said, smiling. 'I can't wait to show Mum I've found her leaf. She'll be so happy.'

As she felt the box lurch once again, sending them into flight, Clara stared in disbelief at how huge the inside of it was. She became wrapped up in its magic once more, all thoughts of tea forgotten.

She felt them spin across the skies, away from the enchanted forest, hurtling through space, until at last it was back in the hide-and-seek woods.

The Doctor brought the ship to a standstill in the same spot where Clara had started to count to a hundred.

She suddenly remembered her friends – they must be so worried. While she'd been off having an adventure they'd probably been searching the woods looking for her. She sprang to the door and pushed it open.

'Thanks for the ride,' she called.

'Nice to meet you again, Clara Oswald.' The Doctor gave her a mysterious look – sort of sad and happy at the same time. 'Now, Clara, listen.'

As she stopped and faced the Doctor, Clara felt that strange sensation again – that she knew this man, somehow.

'So we *have* met before?'

'This is going to sound weird. We'll meet again in the future and have *so many* adventures, I promise, but for now I need you to forget.'

'What?'

He placed a hand on Clara's temple, ever so gently.

'You won't recall any of this trip. You'll forget you ever met me.'

Clara felt like she was falling into a dream, a buzzing sound travelling through her body and brain.

When she opened her eyes, she was in the woods beside a huge oak tree, its branches towering above her into the night sky.

'Come on, Clara.' It was Gem. 'What took you so long? We all got tired of waiting and I came to find *you* instead.'

Clara smiled.

'Where did you get to?' said Ashari, appearing from between the trees.

Clara rubbed her eyes and yawned. 'I don't know what happened. I must have fallen asleep.'

In a daze, her fingers found the leaf and amber nestled in her pocket. For a fleeting moment she remembered something . . . and then, like the best dreams, it flew away into the stars.

VELVET HUGS

KATY MANNING

C losing the front door, I breathed out a huge sigh of contentment and relief – smiling to myself as I surveyed the total devastation that a gaggle of rampaging five-year-olds had created in just three hours. Carefully picking my way through the party debris strewn across the now almost invisible floor, I tripped over a small handmade wooden sledge, setting off a loud jingle from the bells attached. The sledge hit a bright green raptoresque creature that glowed and roared menacingly, reminding me of that Drashig encounter during my early TARDIS-travelling years.

Unsurprisingly, this cacophony disturbed Cliff, who was sprawled out on the sofa, still wearing the smudged remnants of a face painting that I think was meant to be a tiger. Opening one twinkly blue eye, he laughed.

'Oh, Jo, my love. That gathering was almost as exhausting as the weeks we spent in the monkey sanctuary in Zambia.'

He closed his eye again, a smile on his handsome face. I kissed his tiger-painted forehead gently. How I loved this man. And how proud I was of his tireless efforts to protect and preserve this magnificent planet Earth. I chuckled as I recalled our first meeting. Almost a mirror image of my first calamitous encounter with the Doctor. They were so alike in so many ways.

We had just celebrated our second great-grandchild Paulo's fifth birthday. Our enormous and ever-growing family was more than enough for one house, but to this we had temporarily added a herd of little ones. Now they had finally departed, clutching their precious party bags. They would excitedly relate the fun they'd had to their parents, who would now have to cope with their hyper wired wee ones until the sugar rush finally wore off. Much as one might try to avoid them, illicit sugary sweets always sneak their way into children's parties along with plastic gifts that are destined to end up in landfill.

Cliff and I had only just arrived back from a climate change conference in Greenland the day before. Gathering our family together wasn't easy, but several of our beloved tribe had made it, adding to the celebration with love, laughter, boisterous chatter and music. I started the clean-up operation, but then decided to let Cliff rest. I knew he would be planning another impassioned speech for the next conference. Much has been done for climate change, but not nearly enough.

I ambled into the garden, which was another bomb site. The dogs, Grunter and Centauri, were having a field day sniffing out – with tail-wagging glee – rejected squashed cupcakes and anything else that was edible, plus a few things which were definitely not! It was a beautiful English summer evening. The sun was slowly sinking and the sky was a glorious vivid rose pink.

I've always been drawn to this time of the evening, ever since I was a tiny child. I lay down under the huge apple tree, still bearing its sweet-smelling blossoms, while our garden buzzed with drunken bees, enjoying the nectar cocktail hour. Dreamily, I began to recall travelling around Africa with my parents when I was five. I loved the nature there. The exotic trees – the fat-trunked baobab and the Kigelia (the so-called sausage tree). Sustenance and shelter to so much wildlife in Botswana.

My earliest memory is of living in an old abandoned house on the edge of Umtali in Rhodesia, now Zimbabwe.

/

I would stretch out under the giant purple jacaranda tree, listening to nature's twilight concert. The vibrating hum of the heat, the chatter of nesting birds, the drumming of the cicadas rubbing their wings together and the tinkling croak of frogs while the leaves were rustled gently by the grateful whisper of the evening breeze. I used to lie there nearly every evening until bedtime, looking up at the stars through the canopy of deep purple flowers, as the darkening sky covered me with its twinkling starlit black velvet cape. I'd gaze in wonderment, imagining what it would be like to be up there among those stars.

Little did I know that, one day, I would find out.

I didn't have what many would consider a normal education. Instead, I was tutored by my parents as we travelled from place to place. My father was a biological anthropologist (anthropology is the study of humans), and my mother was a nature photographer. I loved going on long walks with her as she took photos of exotic birds and flowers, often running ahead across the rough terrain, fearlessly climbing trees (and anything else that was climbable).

My lessons with them were sporadic, but I read a lot, and my wonderful parents took me on exciting explorations – which was education enough for me. Sometimes we went on thrillingly bumpy trips in our dusty, rusty, rattling old jeep we lovingly called Mildred, on which I had painted enormous multicoloured flowers. I'd spend whole nights sitting in the front seat, looking up at a blaze of stars through the ever-widening holes in her roof.

My childhood freedom meant I could play with the local children in the villages we visited; language never seems to be a barrier with youngsters. We would teach each other games and songs and they would show me how to weave baskets, make pots and identify plants. I would show them the pictures in my favourite books, especially *The Wind in the Willows*, and photographs my mother had taken of me standing proudly with a snowman that I had made during one of our Christmas trips home.

Every Christmas we would return to stay with my Uncle Giles in Dorset, who lived in a grand old mansion surrounded by magical woodlands and rolling hills. Although my parents had a beautiful little cottage on the estate, we always stayed in the mansion with my uncle and his housekeeper of many years, Mrs Baintree (affectionately known as Bainty). I adored these Christmases, especially when it snowed. Uncle Giles had been in the army, and now worked in some sort of secret job which he never spoke about. Even though, as an army man, he had to be stern, he was kind-hearted and loving.

Though, of course, when the imposing grandfather clock struck its seven thunderous chimes I would run as fast as a hunted fox from wherever I had been playing, often sliding down the huge oak bannister (strictly forbidden), skidding into the dining room and landing skilfully on my chair. Lateness was not acceptable in the grand old mansion. After dinner we would gather round a roaring log fire and Uncle Giles would entertain us with thrilling stories of imaginary creatures living on other planets. I would listen in amazement, thinking about the wonders of the universe. After a story he always kissed me goodnight – his mesmerising, perfectly groomed handlebar moustache would tickle my cheek, and I would giggle helplessly.

When I was eight years old and coming to the end of another sublime snowy Christmas in Dorset, I was summoned into the library by Uncle Giles. I loved its scent of polished leather and cigars, which I found strangely comforting. As well as Uncle Giles, my parents were there. They informed me that I was to remain with my uncle and attend a nearby boarding school, as I needed 'a proper education to prepare for a future career', in the words of my uncle. My little heart began to thump heavily in my chest, rare tears burned my eyes. I couldn't speak, my throat was dry and fear ran up my wobbly little legs.

My mother and father hugged me tightly as I choked back my panic, telling me tenderly how this was a wonderful opportunity to meet new friends. My parents promised they would visit me every school holiday, and that it would not be long before they returned to England for good. I clearly remember sobbing myself into a fitful sleep that night.

Waking in the early dawn before anyone else had stirred, I threw on my scarlet hooded dressing gown and oversized boots and made my way to the back of the house and down another set of creaky wooden stairs. I crept into the warm kitchen, sneaking past the sleeping dogs, who blearily acknowledged my presence and carried on dreaming their doggy dreams. I quietly opened the back door and stepped out into the silence of the snow. My eyes still burning with salty tears, I flopped down into the snow, my back against the always-reassuring trunk of my old oak tree, staring up at the sky, which was heavy with an impending snowstorm. I loved and trusted my parents and my uncle. Perhaps they were right. Maybe it was time for a change. Dread it though I might, I had to buck up and be brave. The snow-filled clouds lifted and a hazy sun began to appear. With my new-found determination, I set about building a snowman.

The rest of the holiday passed happily, but all too soon it was time to ready myself for school. Bainty and my mother helped me pack my trunk. According to school rules, my collection of glass-bead necklaces and other cherished trinkets were not classed as essential items! I looked with dismay at my tragic reflection in the mirror. The uniform was drab and itchy and rather large for my tiny frame. A brown tunic, tie, socks and shoes, complete with brown sweater and matching brown bloomers with a pocket, into which I tucked one of the forbidden necklaces. I looked like a bottle of HP brown sauce had been poured over me. I made up my mind there and then that, when I left school, I would never work anywhere that required me to don a uniform.

Boarding school was not an easy time for me. I had never experienced so many strict rules and regulations. No talking in class, in the corridors, or in the dorm after lights out. I broke all of these rules on day one, and had to write out a hundred times, in my neatest handwriting, 'I must not disobey school rules.' Then I had to do it again because the first time I drew a pretty flower at the end of each line.

I had never been a clumsy child, but somehow being in a restricted space, filled with desks and general school clutter, turned me into a walking disaster. Especially in the science lab, where over time I smashed multiple glass test tubes and knocked over a Bunsen burner, causing a small fire. The fire was actually rather exciting, until I was sent to the headmistress's office for a gruelling lecture on my foolhardy behaviour.

I tried my hardest in every subject, I really did. But my first school report was pretty awful, and they didn't improve from there. The headmistress wrote: 'Josephine is a bright girl, popular with the other pupils and always ready to help anyone in difficulties. She has a strong sense of fair play but must learn to control her impulsiveness and at times reckless behaviour. Josephine's continuing misdemeanours cannot go unpunished and will only hold her back from becoming a good student with a promising future.'

Somehow, I miraculously managed not to be expelled. But the next disappointment was my GCE results. I only scraped through with a few passes. And I failed all of my A levels. If getting into trouble and breaking rules had been a subject, I would have, in today's language, 'smashed it'!

With this discouraging end to my schooling, I was worried that I had disappointed those who loved me. But my parents were really cool about it. What surprised me most, though, was my Uncle Giles's reaction. He seemed completely unbothered. He called me into the library, which still held the faint scent of leather and cigars but, strangely, now with the added intoxicating fragrance of patchouli. He sat me down and explained that he knew what I needed to do and that he would arrange everything for me. My future, he told me, with a hint of a smile under his now greying and slightly thinning moustache, was assured. I wanted to ask what 'my future' was, but he just looked into my eyes.

'It's your destiny, JoJo. It's where you will meet the most important person in your life. A person who will teach you, guide you, and take you on unimaginable adventures.'

With that, he stubbed out his cigar, gave me a moustachioed, cheek-tickling kiss and left. *Gosh*, I thought, *what was in that cigar?* I trusted my uncle and appreciated his help, but *I* was going to be in charge of my own destiny, thank you very much!

That evening, I was lying in my familiar spot under the ancient oak tree, watching the sun gradually sink behind the hills, bidding the day goodnight. Suddenly a delicious waft of patchouli drifted past my nostrils, followed by a huge plume of smoke.

'Hello, Josephine, luvvy,' a raspy northern-accented voice said. I sat up, thinking I had fallen asleep and was still in the shadow of a dream. But as I lifted my head, I was immediately transfixed by piercing blue eyes, surrounded by

pearlescent eye shadow. I blinked in disbelief as I focused
on the woman's matching purple hair and strings of
kaleidoscopic glass beads. On top of this psychedelic haze
sat an impossibly outlandish hat, festooned with feathers.
I opened my mouth to speak but nothing came out.

'It's all right, Jo, love, I just popped by to assure you that
your ever-so-handsome Uncle Giles is right, chuck. Trust him,
and me, your old Auntie Iris Wildthyme. You will travel
among those stars you always dream of when you look up at
that wondrous universe, safe in the hands of someone that
will exhilarate you, nurture you, and introduce you to untold
adventures on other planets far from this one. It will change
your young understanding of life forever, chuck.'

I managed to squeeze one breathy word out of my
gawping mouth: 'Who . . .'

'Exactly,' she said, hugging me tightly. And with a swoosh
of fake leopard skin and vivid green fur she was gone.

I told my uncle about this curious encounter with –
what had she called herself? – Auntie Iris, over dinner that
night. He just smiled enigmatically, poured me my very first
glass of wine, and simply said that soon all would be
made abundantly clear. And that I should listen to her very
wise words.

*

My parents returned for my nineteenth birthday. We had a party filled with army people adorned with gleaming medals, and a few close school chums of mine. After a delicious dinner – which even Bainty attended, looking more glamorous and younger than I had ever seen her – the lights were dimmed and a gigantic cake in the shape of a star, glowing with candles, was carried in. I blew out all nineteen candles in one puff and made my secret wish. Then to the garden, where a little stage had been erected and illuminated by hundreds of fairy lights. Four gorgeous boys (bearing an uncanny resemblance to the Liverpool lads themselves) played their way through a long list of Beatles songs. They finished with one of my favourites, 'I Am the Walrus'. It was the grooviest, most fantabulous birthday ever and one I would never forget.

When the grandfather clock struck its last midnight-booming chime I bid fond farewells to everyone and within moments the house had emptied, as if by magic. I was elated as I lay under the knowing old oak tree, savouring the stupendous evening and beholding the bewitching beauty of the autumnal sky. I swear I even saw an impossible red double-decker bus flash across the heavens like a shooting star! Though maybe the glass of champagne had gone to my head . . .

*

The next day, Bainty, once again looking like the familiar grandmotherly figure I knew and adored, helped me pack, even letting me take my glass beads and newly acquired collection of rings. Looking at myself in the long mirror, I recalled seeing my reflection as an eight-year-old in the hideous brown school uniform that was now, thankfully, abandoned. I felt relieved that my new outfit was at least cheery and totally on trend. Packing done, I went outside to say a sad goodbye to my dear, reassuring old friend of so many years, hugging its broad gnarled trunk. Moments later, a sleek, highly polished car with blacked-out windows pulled up to the house. A rather good-looking young man in army uniform got out and stood to attention by the passenger door. I bid my cherished family farewell and slid into the back seat, heading into the thrill of the unknown.

I couldn't see through the blacked-out windows and the panel between me and the driver was also darkly tinted and opaque, obliterating any clues as to where I was going. It was all a little disarming. My earlier courage started to falter, and large butterflies began to flap their wings inside my tummy as we drove towards my inexplicable, unknown destiny. After about an hour or so the car's engine stopped purring and I felt us begin to drop, as if the car was being lowered into the bowels of the earth. Then there was a huge clunk, followed by the sound of metal doors clanking open. My good-looking but silent driver ushered me into a small room with a bed and only the bare necessities.

I waited nervously until I was escorted down some very bland, winding corridors to an office where a charming gentleman introduced himself as Brigadier Alistair Lethbridge-Stewart. He welcomed me courteously and explained what I was about to embark on.

'You are now a trainee with a secret branch of the army known as UNIT: United Nations Intelligence Taskforce. You will remain here for a year's training, in readiness for a rather special assignment as a fully qualified agent. Oh, and, Miss Grant, I do hope you make a good cup of tea.'

Tea, I thought. Is that it? One thing I *was* grateful for, though, was that I was not expected to wear a uniform, as I certainly didn't believe a disciplined army life was for me. Surely after all the incredible things I had been told, this couldn't be the exciting but mysterious, life-altering future I had been promised?

But life-altering it was. Over the next year – and it absolutely was a year – I was trained in safe-breaking and explosives (well, I thought, if I didn't succeed here I could always take up bank robbery), cryptology and karate and general self-defence. I threw myself into it all with much enthusiasm, especially the assault courses, and only had a few minor mishaps along the way.

When my training came to an end, the Brigadier called me into his office. I entered with trepidation, fingers crossed behind my back, hoping with every fibre of my being that I had passed. I knocked nervously on the door. The Brigadier bid me enter.

'Good morning, Miss Grant. I trust you slept well?' The Brigadier didn't wait for a response. 'Congratulations, I am pleased to inform you that you have successfully completed your training course. With, I am delighted to say, flying colours. You are now a fully qualified member of UNIT. Well done.'

I wanted to throw my arms round him with sheer delight. But I knew this was not *quite* the right way of showing my elation to the commanding officer of UNIT, so I just grinned and thanked him (perhaps a little too profusely). Picking up his leather gloves and cap, the impeccably turned-out Brigadier opened the door, indicating that we were done.

'You will now begin your first assignment as assistant to the Doctor. A splendid fellow, if a little eccentric, but you will soon find all of that out. Down the corridor, third door on the left. Good luck, Miss Grant.' A cryptic smile emerged from beneath his neat moustache. Lifting one perfect eyebrow, he added, 'You may need it.' With that, he exited and marched down the corridor.

I stood there for a moment, incredulous. Doctor? Yikes. I knew nothing about medicine apart from a smattering of plant remedies. And nothing on my course had anything to do with medicine! I walked slowly down the dimly lit corridor, pondering this, and the words of my uncle and strange Auntie Iris. Then I reached the door. A sign said SCIENCE LABORATORY in large letters. My heart sank, remembering my catastrophic days in the school laboratory. All I could hope for was that UNIT had a continuous supply of test tubes and a fire extinguisher! I took a deep, fortifying breath and, with all the bravado I could muster, I knocked on the door . . .

I was awoken from this memory by a sudden choking sound, followed by long wheezing whistles. I jumped to my feet, wondering what planet I was on and what alien I was about to face. Then I saw Grunter hunched over, heaving and convulsing. I sped to his side, frantic with fear. The plastic end of a party whizzer was wedged in his gullet, and every time he coughed the paper tube unfurled like a giant lizard's tongue, emitting a wet, discordant hissing sound.

Speedily and carefully, if with some difficulty, I managed to remove it. And after a couple of bone-shaking retches, and a few soothing hugs from me, Grunter seemed to recover from his near-death experience. He bounded off towards the pond, followed by a playful Centauri. I heard Cliff calling me, and hid the offending plastic contraband. The last thing I needed was for Cliff to have an outburst about the environmental damage done by plastic.

'Jo, my love,' he said in his lilting Welsh voice, 'your red-alert phone is beeping.'

It could only be Kate Stewart, daughter of Brigadier Alistair Lethbridge-Stewart, a truly remarkable woman and chief scientific officer of UNIT, now renamed the United Intelligence Taskforce. Her father would have been so proud of her. I still miss him.

I had been called in several times to help UNIT, which always gladdened my heart. I could never imagine losing that part of my life.

I kissed my darling Nobel-Peace-Prize-winning environmental hero of a husband gently on the lips.

'See you in Norway,' I said. 'Unless the TARDIS returns me to some Norse God debacle.'

Cliff scooped me into his arms. 'Well, *Fy nghariad*, if you do end up there, say hello to Odin for me. And no lying under the Sacred Old Ash tree!'

On the way to the UNIT base I began to think about my Doctor. Although I had seen several regenerations over the years, I knew that whatever their outer shell looked like, the two hearts that beat within belonged to the same compassionate, solitary genius. Someone who only ever sought truth, justice and peace throughout the universe. I will never lose the memory of the safe certainty that came from his velvet hugs, while I looked up at his strong, noble, fine face, and into his wonderfully understanding eyes. Eyes that held fathomless lifetimes, but always a tinge of sadness. My Doctor, who I have loved unceasingly, is etched into my heart forever. Until I reach the end of my human days and depart on my last awfully big adventure.

DÉJÀ DONNA

SARAH DANIELS

D onna pushes open the door of the TARDIS, steps out into a crowded street and has to dodge the shoppers bustling by. She's confronted by a lofty building of girders and glass, and a train clatters along a railway bridge nearby, forcing pigeons into the air. She cranes her neck to read the stark black letters that stretch above the entrance.

'Borough Market? Well, that's . . . underwhelming,' she says.

'You said, "surprise me". So here you go – surprise,' the Doctor says, hopping down from the TARDIS. He shoves his hands into his trouser pockets. 'Where were you expecting?'

'Don't know,' Donna says. She gazes at the busy London Street. 'When a spaceman says, "let's go for a bite to eat", you kind of expect them to take advantage of the *being able to travel through the whole of space and time* thing. Not take you somewhere you can get to on the Jubilee Line.'

'You'll be surprised what's here if you take time to look,' the Doctor replies. He marches into the glass-roofed building. 'Come on then,' he shouts over his shoulder.

Donna runs to catch up.

Inside, the market is crammed with shoppers, the air heavy with the scents of caramel and fried bacon. The Doctor leads Donna between lines of canary-yellow canopies. At the far end of the market they pass under an arch held up by green-and-gold girders and enter a part of the market Donna doesn't remember visiting before.

'This is where you find the more interesting stuff,' the Doctor says with a mischievous smile.

'Looks just like any other market if you ask me. Food carts. Knock-off cleaning supplies. Second-hand stuff they re-label as *vintage*.'

'Well, yes, on the surface. But have a real look,' the Doctor says.

Donna scans the nearest stall. It's a table piled high with second-hand kids' clothes. Socks rolled into balls. Battered trainers held in pairs by elastic bands. The woman behind the table glares at the Doctor like he's trouble. Her blonde hair is piled on top of her head in a '60s beehive and her fringe skims a cloud of dots where her eyebrows should be. Realisation washes over Donna. 'Interesting tattoos,' she says.

'She's Drahvin. And not all that friendly,' the Doctor says.

'A Drah-what?'

'*Shhhhh!* She's going incognito. It's only polite to play along.' He herds Donna away from the woman and her stall. Once they're out of earshot, the Doctor stops in the middle of a wide aisle between stalls.

'What's she doing here?' Donna asks.

'Selling overpriced kids' clothes by the looks of it.'

'No, what's she doing here. In London. On Earth?'

'Good question. Have a look around.'

Donna turns a circle, looking from stall to stall. She clocks a broad-necked man with no hair who's trundling past, pulling a shopping basket on wheels. As he walks further away, Donna notices there are only three fingers clasped round the trolley's handle. 'Wait, he's Sontaran.'

'He is. Might be a tourist trying out Earth for a day. Most humans are too busy and too closed-minded to notice. They see something strange and their brain kind of blurs it out – especially if it means reworking their understanding of the entire universe.'

Donna takes a few steps towards the nearest stall. It's cluttered with old clocks and fireplace brushes coated in coal dust. Behind the stall, a woman with a silver-grey perm and a deeply wrinkled face smiles kindly. Donna runs her hand through a box of coins, and the iron-y smell coats her fingers. 'You've shown me some things, spaceman, but this one's got me gobsmacked. Exactly how many aliens are there in London?'

The Doctor shrugs. 'Hard to say. A smattering. Most of them head here when they arrive. The market's a good place for them to hide and there's already aliens here to help them get settled.'

'Not here to invade, are they?' Donna says under her breath.

'Course not. Well, not most of them anyway. Can never be too sure about the Drahvins.' The Doctor looks over his shoulder as if he's checking no one can hear him. 'No, most of this lot are just working, building lives, looking for somewhere safe to spend their days. It happens the same all over the galaxy. Whether it's a failed harvest, or an interplanetary conflict, or a star swallowing its own solar system – when your home isn't safe anymore you have to start over somewhere else.'

Donna's eye catches on a postcard propped up between a dented tankard and someone's school swimming trophy.

Her memory prickles. She picks the postcard up and stares at the sepia tone image of Chiswick High Street. 'I've got the strangest feeling of déjà vu,' she whispers, almost to herself.

'You can have that, dear,' the old stallholder says, 'in exchange for a handshake.'

'Very kind of you,' Donna says. Without taking her eyes off the postcard, she reaches over the stall to the woman's outstretched hand.

'Oh, no, you don't.' The Doctor jostles Donna before she makes contact with the woman's hand. 'We'll have no cloning today, thank you very much,' he says, still pushing Donna away from the stall.

Looking back, Donna realises with a snap of horror what's going on. Where the hand was a second before, there's now a fleshy, suckered tentacle reaching after her. 'What was that?'

'That was a Zygon and it was about to become *you*. Might as well have a big neon sign above your head flashing *tourist, feel free to scam me.*'

Donna slides the postcard into her pocket, but as she follows the Doctor through the market she can feel it sitting there, niggling at her like an old scar. *It's a coincidence,* she tells herself. *It's a mass-produced image. One of thousands of identical*

DOCTOR WHO: ORIGIN STORIES

postcards that are sold all over London. There's zero chance this is the same postcard I remember.

Three stalls later, the Doctor stops, takes a large pastry from a wobbling pyramid of them and holds it out to the stallholder – a small man with wavy brown hair and eyes set wide in his face. The man hovers his hand over the pastry, and a thick, yellowish liquid drizzles from each finger on to the food. 'Thanks very much,' the Doctor says, taking the pastry. 'I won't shake hands.'

'Suit yourself. Don't get many of your kind down this end of the market,' the man says. He presents another pastry to Donna.

'Looks like honey,' Donna says, inspecting the serviette-wrapped treat.

'Something like that.' The Doctor grins and takes a bite.

'It'd be more appetising if he hadn't stuck his fingers in it first.'

'Come on, Donna. Be brave.'

Donna feels her smile drop. 'All these beings living in London – right under my nose – and I never even realised. I could've chatted to them at the bus stop, eaten their food, lived next door to them. I just persuaded myself there was a normal, Earth-based explanation for them.'

292

The Doctor chews, watching her. 'Well, you didn't notice the Sycorax and that was a full-scale invasion. Chances are you've met more than a few non-Earth beings in your life without realising it. Come on, I fancy something for the road.' The Doctor drops the last bit of pastry into a bin and marches towards a coffee cart. By the time Donna gets there, he's already ordered them both huge cardboard cups of frothy coffee. Donna watches shoppers milling about through the steam as she sips, trying to spot which are human and which are not. Trawling her memory for others she might have missed.

'Penny for them,' the Doctor says finally.

Donna takes a shuddering breath. 'Something happened when I was a kid. There was this place – this cave – and there was a legend about it. Sounds silly now I'm saying it out loud . . . but it was about the cave eating kids.'

'Sounds utterly terrifying,' the Doctor says, and Donna can tell by the glee in his eyes that he's being sarcastic.

'It was, actually. Still gives me the heebie-jeebies thinking about what happened that night. Now you've got me wondering whether there was something non-Earthly about it. What if there really was a carnivorous . . . *thing*, down there?'

The Doctor looks at her under his eyebrows, clearly unconvinced.

Donna slides the postcard from her pocket. 'I saw this postcard twenty years ago. I could've died that night and I'd like to know if there was some daft alien behind it all.'

What if this is the same postcard? she thinks without asking the question out loud.

'If only we had a time machine. We could nip back and check,' the Doctor says.

'Really?'

'No, not really.' He tuts. 'Of course we can't. Because what's the first rule of time travel, Donna Noble?'

'Never go to Grallista Social on a bank holiday weekend,' Donna says, and she can't help grinning despite the topic of conversation.

'Well. Yes. But what else?'

'Never cross your own timeline.'

'Never cross your own timeline,' the Doctor repeats.

'Go on. It'll be five minutes. Just long enough for you to use one of your gadgets to check whether there's an alien sitting in the bottom of that cave.'

'What is it with humans and urban legends? Every bridge has a troll; every old house has a ghost. Nine times out of ten there's nothing unusual going on at all. And even when there is more to a story, sometimes it's best to let sleeping aliens lie. Why do you want to go back so much all of a sudden?'

Donna shrugs. 'Being here with all these aliens hidden in plain sight made me wonder what others I've missed.'

The Doctor considers Donna. She can tell he's trying to make a decision. 'Promise you won't try to interact with your younger self.'

Donna feels herself break into a broad smile. 'Scout's honour,' she says. 'And once we've checked it out, we can come back and get as many disgusting pastries covered in alien goop as you want.'

Donna's going to show that Marcus Shaw what for.

As soon as the final lesson ended, she started following him and she's already trailed him from the school gate, down two streets with houses on either side and over the canal bridge, ignoring the splash of puddle water that soaked through her school tights. Her ears are burning with rage, and her fingers are scrunched into each other so tight she can't unfurl them.

She stomps down the curve of pavement that leads through the wooded bit by the canal, kicking a Vimto can out of the way. The air is heavy with the threat of rain, and the ground is swampy underfoot. It's been raining solidly for three days, and now there are mini streams weaving their way down through the trees. Rivulets cross the footpaths, and the place is alive with the sound of running water.

Everyone in Year Nine is calling her Little Miss Bossy, and it's all because of Marcus Shaw. Two weeks ago they'd had to work together on the Bunsen burners (one pair per Bunsen), and by the time they were ready to start their experiment that idiot had burned through every scrap of magnesium ribbon they had. She was forced to go and ask Miss Frakes for more, and when she got back she told Marcus – categorically – *not to set it alight.*

'All right, Little Miss Bossy,' he'd said so loud that everyone stopped what they were doing and turned to look at them. She had felt herself turning a bright shade of beetroot while he sat there sneering. Everyone else was sniggering and poking each other in the ribs, barely containing themselves, so that in the end Miss Frakes had shouted, 'Enough!'

Ever since, it's been relentless. Marcus takes every chance he gets to tease her. What's more, he manages to whip the rest of the class up too. Miss Frakes even said if Marcus put half as much effort into his homework as he did into tormenting Donna he'd be a straight-A student.

By the time she spots Marcus on the footpath ahead of her, it's raining again and getting darker by the minute. She reaches back and clicks on the torch that she always has dangling from the top zip of her schoolbag.

Donna *is* bossy when she needs to be – she knows that. But she's been trying to rein it in; trying to shake off that part of herself and be more fun, so that it'll be easier for the class to like her. She's even stopped herself grabbing the pen when it's time for note-taking during group work (although her handwriting is *definitely* the neatest). Now Marcus Shaw has ruined it, and 'bossy' is going to follow her for months. In fact, someone's already graffitied one of the toilet stalls with a little blue cartoon character next to the words *Donna Noble A.K.A Little Miss Bossy* and a fat arrow in black marker. Marcus Shaw's the one who's spreading it. So he's the one that can stop it too.

'Oi, Shaw!' she shouts. She doesn't know what she's planning to do: just talk to him, probably. She jogs faster and realises they're coming to the part of the path that goes right past The Cave – an outcrop of dark sandstone full of cracks and openings and places to fall into. She wouldn't usually walk this way. Everyone at school knows kids go missing near that cave. It doesn't matter how many times her mum tells her she's being silly for believing the stories. Last summer, a group of Year Tens carried a mirror down into the cave, saying they were going to play Bloody Mary. A crowd gathered outside to watch. After five minutes, the ones that had gone in came running out, screaming, saying something was in the wall and had tried to snatch them. They were all pale and sweaty.

Donna had promised herself she wouldn't go in there. Ever.

He's just ahead of her now, and she's sure he's ignoring her shouts, which makes her even more infuriated. 'Marcus, you come back here!' Donna hollers, breaking into a trot. Her heart's beating now – part anger, part anticipation, part adrenaline. She can feel the heat creeping up her neck.

He stops and spins round. 'What do you want, Noble? I've got to be on my paper round by half-past four and I'm already late. Don't need you slowing me down,' he says.

'I think the world will keep turning if you're ten minutes late with the evening news, Marcus.'

Here, the rainwater runs down a steep hill, across the footpath and into the mouth of the cave. The opening is blocked by a black gate, and there's a big yellow sign with a picture of a stick figure falling into waves: KEEP OUT – DEEP WATER.

Marcus shifts his bag on one strap, a half-eaten bag of Wotsits clutched in his fist. He's got no coat, even though it's pouring it down, and his hair's all stuck to his forehead. His shirt tails are sticking out from under his school sweatshirt, and Donna notices now that the knee of his trousers has a puckered line where his mum's sewn a hole together.

Donna ignores the prickly feeling on the back of her neck that that being this close to The Cave gives her. She ignores the fact that the shadows around the entrance seem to go the wrong way, and the way the gate sways in the corner of her eye. She focuses on Marcus.

'What have you been saying about me?' Donna says.

Marcus tips the remaining Wotsits into his mouth and scrunches up the packet, dropping it into the puddle at his feet.

'Nothing,' Marcus says, sniffing and rubbing the end of his nose with cheese-stained fingers. 'Nothing that's not true, anyway.' He smirks.

'Look, stop calling me that name, all right? If you stop saying it, everyone else will stop too.'

'What name?' he says, innocently.

Donna huffs in frustration. 'Stop calling me "Little Miss Bossy",' she says through gritted teeth. She wipes rainwater off her face.

'OK, OK, Little Miss Boss–' Marcus starts to say, before cutting himself off. 'No need to get your knickers in a twist.' He raises his hands, and his eyebrows, in mock surrender, then looks over at the cave entrance. Above them, the single street lamp pings on, dropping eerie, colourless light on to the rock face. 'Tell you what – dare you to go in there for one whole minute and I promise I'll drop it.'

A cold wave of dread washes over Donna. But instead of backing away, she takes a step towards Marcus. He's quite a lot bigger than her, and as she looks up into his face he makes no attempt to hide his amusement.

'You might be able to bully everyone else in the year – but I'm not scared of you,' Donna says. She wishes her voice wasn't coming out wobbly.

He leans closer so that Donna catches a faint whiff of Wotsit breath. 'Maybe you should be,' he says. A flash of lightning picks out Marcus's heavy brow ridges and hollow cheeks.

Donna turns her face away so that Marcus can't see how nervous she is and waves a hand in front of her nose. 'Phew, should probably lay off those cheesy crisps, mate.'

A ripple of rage crosses Marcus's face. Without warning, he grabs the strap of her school bag and drags it from her shoulder. In a second, he's striding off towards the cave, sloshing through the rivulet that runs into the darkness, the torch attached to Donna's bag swinging wildly. He pulls the gate of the cave until it clangs against the chain holding it closed, then squeezes underneath the gap he's created, carrying Donna's schoolbag with him.

Donna's gut tells her to run away. It's not worth going

into the cave after Marcus Shaw. Not even to retrieve the new schoolbag that she only got at the start of term. Not even to fetch her half-written history essay still inside the bag. She stands frozen in the rain.

Then she ducks under the chain and follows Marcus into the darkness.

Once inside, Donna clings to the gate like a life preserver. It's so cold that her fingers ache. The cave's roof has collapsed in places, letting dingy moonlight stream in. Thick tree roots grow through the rock, dripping with rainwater. Beneath her feet the ground slopes downwards, water flowing over it – so much so that her knees are splashed.

'Marcus?' she calls. Her voice is thin. There's no sign of him.

In the darkness, Donna makes out an arch where the walls of the cave have been reinforced with the same kind of brick they built the canals out of. She keeps her fingers clasped round the gate . . . and is still holding on to it when a scream tears through the darkness. A scream so loud and shrill she's sure it was a cry of death.

Donna opens the door of the TARDIS and finds the rain thrashing down, exactly the way she remembers it on that day, the sky slate-grey and angry. She jumps out without hesitation.

The Doctor brought the TARDIS down right on top of the exposed rock and now Donna has to pick her way along, stepping from boulder to boulder. She ignores the way the loose rocks and pebbles slip out from under her feet, the creaking and shifting sounds that join the rain. In seconds she touches down on to the tufty, sodden grass and then on to the footpath. It's like walking through a dream. Donna remembers every detail, from the smell of the rain to a gut-thumping crash of thunder, and as she turns a corner and strides towards the cave's entrance she knows exactly what she'll see. Herself and Marcus Shaw in the last argument they ever had.

'Don't get too close!' She ignores the Doctor's call from somewhere behind her.

Donna sees her now. A young girl, red hair tied in a ponytail; schoolbag carried by one strap with the little torch shining at the top; her fingers clenched at her side. There's rainwater flowing over the path, carrying crisp packets and last autumn's leaves down into the cave's entrance so that they pile up against the black bars of the gate. Donna remembers the intensity of the confrontation, the way it felt like the anger was going to burst out of her. She sees herself square up to Marcus Shaw, and then watches as he gets in her face the second before he snatches her bag.

Lightning flashes above the outcrop. Donna watches

herself trying to decide whether to follow Marcus through the gate and into the cave. *The place that makes children disappear.* She wipes water from her face.

The Doctor pulls Donna into the shadows behind a rock, out of sight of Donna's younger self. They lean back, breathing heavily. 'This is too risky,' he says.

There's a scream from inside the cave – the strangled noise of someone in real trouble. The Doctor's eyes widen. 'That didn't sound good.'

Donna peers round the rock. Her younger self is now frozen in place, her hand on the gate. Donna remembers being paralysed by fear; how her tears mixed with the rain on her cheeks, how her ponytail was soaked and hanging heavily down her back.

Donna starts to leave their hiding place, but the Doctor holds her back. 'Sorry, can't let you do it.'

'*You* go out and help her – me – then!'

'I can't. We didn't meet, did we? You'd have recognised me.'

'No, you don't understand. She's – I'm – whatever – not going to help him!'

'What?'

Donna's shaking her head so hard that the rain flies from her hair. She balls her fists. There's guilt swelling through her, even after all these years. 'There's a kid down there. And right now, that young girl is going to let him die. I was too scared. There was too much water. And all that stuff about the kids disappearing. I was standing there, absolutely freezing, and terrified, and one hundred per cent sure that those stories about the cave eating kids were real. There was no way I was going in that cave.'

'Don't believe you. I know you, Donna, and you'd never let someone – a kid – get hurt if there's a way you can help them.'

Donna presses her lips together to stop herself crying. She looks at the ground. 'Now, maybe. But not then. It was too scary back then. I wasn't brave.'

The Doctor looks at her. Finally, he says, 'Nope. Not buying it. You were already Donna, even back then. Courageous right down to your bones and just as headstrong.'

'I was just a kid, Doctor.'

'So what happened back then? What gave you the nudge you needed to be a hero? Because it certainly wasn't bumping into a time-travelling version of yourself.'

Donna pulls the postcard of Chiswick High Street from her pocket. Raindrops soak into the card. 'I think it was me.'

Thirteen-year-old Donna sprints from the cave entrance, the scream echoing inside her head. The mud seems to be sucking her back, clinging to her school shoes, dragging her further into the cave. When she makes it to the trees she holds on. The water is a torrent now, full of mud and sticks and rubbish. It's too much. If she lets go, she'll be pulled into the water and down into the cave and never found. She can't save Marcus. Can't even try. She's just a kid; a nobody. Little Miss Bossy. Even if she runs up to the High Street and finds a copper – or anyone who can help – Marcus will be floating face down in a pool of mud by the time the help arrives. All she can do is cling to this tree until the rain stops.

There's a thud. Donna looks down. Half a brick has landed at her feet, clumsily wrapped in a piece of soggy card. Ignoring the water flowing around her, she crouches against the tree to pick the brick up. Her fingers shake as she unwraps the wet card. On one side, a yellowish picture of Chiswick High Street in the olden days. She turns it over and presses the crumpled edges out. In black handwriting, the ink already weeping and spreading, are the words: *BE BRAVE.*

Donna drops the brick and looks around, but there's only shadows and rain. She doesn't know where the message came from, or if the words were meant for her. She turns to face the cave. Determination overpowers her fear, the fire of it burning against the icy rain. She retraces her steps, ducking through the gate and under the half-collapsed ceiling of the cave until she's standing beneath the brick-built archway.

'Donna!' Marcus's voice comes out of the darkness.

Donna clings to the side of the archway while her eyes adjust to the dim light. The noise of rushing water clammers around her and seems to get louder by the second. Just centimetres in front of her, the sloping floor gives way to a short, steep ramp lined with smooth cobbles. At the end of the ramp there's a drop, and Donna can hear water churning somewhere below. In the dank light she makes out other openings in the walls and ceiling, all bringing fast-flowing water into the chamber. 'A storm drain,' she mutters to herself. She knows from her history lessons that these drains were built by the Victorians to gather water from all around, channelling it downwards until it gets deposited in the canal. They weren't made for people, so they didn't think too much about how someone might get out again if they were unlucky enough to fall in. She realises now that the stories were true – kids did go missing down here. But there was no monster. A steep drop and a bad storm and someone could get lost down here without anyone ever knowing to look for them. And now she's going missing too. Tree roots straggle from the roof of the cave, dropping clods of earth. She can taste mud and adrenaline with every breath. The pull is real; everything falls downwards. *Don't panic*, she tells herself. *Save it for after*. 'Marcus! Where are you?' she shouts.

'I fell down here! It's too high, I can't climb out.'

Donna leans forwards as far as she dares, fingernails clinging to the wet brick. What she sees makes her heart plummet. Marcus is standing in water up to his chest, with no way to climb out. The drop isn't much higher than him, but without a foothold or something to climb up, it might as well be a mile downwards.

Donna's mind wheels through options. If she can somehow reach him, she might be able to pull Marcus out.

She lies down on the bricks in the archway and stretches to Marcus. She crushes the fear that she's going to slide forward and end up with Marcus in black, swirling water. Their fingers touch, but the rain and mud make them too slick to get a good grip. 'Throw me my bag!' she shouts over the noise of the torrent. Marcus is shaking with cold. In the darkness his face looks bone white.

'No, you're going to leave me!' he shouts, and now she sees how scared he is. His face is all tight with fear and it feels like her heart is going to shatter.

'I won't, I promise.' Donna hesitates, trying to figure out how to make Marcus trust her. 'And I think I can get you out, but you've got to let me boss you around, OK? Now, throw me the bag.'

There's silence from below. Finally, her bag swings over

the edge of the slope. Donna misses it once, twice, then manages to grab it. Moving as fast as her freezing fingers will let her, she unclips the straps of the bag and lets them unfurl, praying that the cheap nylon bag her mum bought her from Borough Market will be strong enough to hold Marcus's weight. She needs something to attach the bag to, and her heart gives a giddy leap when she spots a sturdy tree root growing up through the brick floor on the other side of the arch. Just as quickly, she realises the bag is too short to reach Marcus, even with the straps dangling from it like a rope.

'You still there?' Marcus shouts up. There's a creaking sound from above them. Water's running through the ceiling now, bringing clods of earth and rotten bricks splashing down with it. 'Donna?!'

Donna can feel the place coming down around them, moving with the pressure of the storm water. She needs to act. Without thinking, she unbuckles her belt, loops it through the tree root and around her ankle, fastening it as tight as her hands can pull. She lies down flat on the brick, wraps one strap of the bag around her hand, and throws the other end down to Marcus. 'Grab on!' she shouts. As soon as she feels Marcus's weight on the bag, she pulls. He weighs a tonne. His feet slip out from under him as he tries to find a foothold in the wet wall. A brick comes loose from the edge and thumps down into the darkness below. Donna can see water running in between the bricks now, little spurts and new streams emerging right out of the slope. The whole thing's going to be washed away – and they'll go with it.

The belt looped around Donna's ankle creaks, the root of the tree stretching. She closes her eyes tight and holds her breath. If it snaps, she'll be down there with Marcus. She can tell the leather on her shoes is all scratched and, even now, facing death, it flashes through her mind that her mum's going to kill her.

It feels as if she's hauling him up for an eternity before she finally hears Marcus's ragged breathing by her face. She grabs him by the back of his shirt collar and pulls. Then they're heaving each other away from the edge of the slope. Her foot slips free from the belt with alarming ease, making her stomach lurch. It was the only thing keeping her secure.

Then they're running together out of the cave, sloshing through the rainwater until they're suddenly in the open air. She's breathing so hard that her chest groans with pain and her fingers feel like they've got ice under the skin. Then Donna trips, faceplanting into the mud. From the ground she sees Marcus stop to look at her, and then he's gone.

Donna rolls on to her back and breathes in the wet air. The rain has suddenly stopped. Stars peek out between the clouds. Her heart's fluttering, and now that the adrenaline is leaching from her body, she feels stretched and thin.

The wind seems to intensify, howling around the rocky outcrop of the cave and filling the night with an unnatural rhythmic whooshing. The sound of masonry and boulders crashing into water signals the final collapse of the ancient storm drain.

'Well, that was interesting,' the Doctor says. He grabs a towel from one of the handrails in the console room and rubs his hair with it, then throws it at Donna. 'You promised you wouldn't get involved.'

'I'm in trouble, aren't I?' Donna says.

'Nah. No harm done. Was it always your plan to throw that brick?'

'Not a plan exactly. More a hunch – that it was the same postcard I'd seen all those years ago, and that somehow it needed to get back to the '80s. I never knew where it'd come from.'

'Until now.' The Doctor scans the strange writing on the central control console. 'No aliens, either, according to the TARDIS. Just a couple of stupid kids and some crumbling Victorian drainage pipes.'

'Oi! Who you calling stupid?'

The Doctor grins. 'What happened to Marcus after? Was your friendship forged in fire? Or in this case, icy storm water?'

Donna sighs and shrugs. 'He refused to talk to me. Think he was embarrassed that he needed rescuing. Stopped calling me "Little Miss Bossy" though, so that's a silver lining. Then he changed schools and I never saw him again. Funny thing though, I was lying there on the ground thanking my lucky stars that I was still alive, and then the whole thing just came crashing down.'

'Yeah, funny that. Shall we change the subject?'

'It was us, wasn't it? I made you bring us back, and you landed the TARDIS on top of that rickety old storm drain and that's what made the whole thing collapse.'

'Look, the storm and the fact that it was built a hundred-and-fifty years ago didn't help with the structural integrity of the place. It was just a matter of time until the whole thing caved in.'

'But it was us that made it go that night. It might have lasted another hundred-and-fifty years without a spaceship landing smack bang on top of it. And I strong-armed you into it, didn't I? It's my fault. I messed everything up. Again.'

'If you hadn't been there to send yourself that note, Marcus might not have made it out alive. You were – you *are* – brilliant. A force of nature. Still a kid and you already committed an act of bravery and selflessness most humans will never accomplish in their entire lives. All it took was telling yourself you could do it.'

Donna feels heat rising to her cheeks. She allows herself a smile and turns to the console. She rests her hands on the controls. 'Can I drive?'

'Well – '

'Come on. You said I was brilliant. Let me drive.'

'I don't think – '

'Force of nature, you said.'

'All right, don't let it go to your head. Tell you what, let's get some proper food, then I'll give you a driving lesson somewhere that you're not going to crash into anything important.'

Donna breaks into a grin.

'So, where do you want to eat?' the Doctor says. 'I know this great little place in Rome. And it definitely *will* be Rome this time.'

'I want to go to Borough Market, obviously. After all that danger I feel like being brave and coming face to face with some aliens.'

EPILOGUE: TEMPERED

DAVE RUDDEN

*T*hey come for the boy at sundown.

     He has dined lightly, as per Academy tradition. Smoked magenta seeds — something simple to line his stomach. It is a long, hard walk to the caldera. Some children fall to exhaustion before they even make it halfway and must be carried back to live with the shame forever.

Not me, *the boy thinks with the pure and terrible certainty of the young, as the Time Lords enter the room, their faces set and grim.* I'm special.

The first clue Foyo Vedrashimeen had to his impending demise was when the moon exploded.

     'It's odd, isn't it?' he said, leaning forward and tapping a screen. 'Hard copy of those scans, please.'

His TARDIS responded with a pulse of light down its control column, setting the red glass aflame like a Gallifreyan sunrise. With a warble, pages began to feed from an ornate slot above the console. It was a weakness, he knew, as he reached out to snag one of the falling pages before it hit the floor. There was no limit to a TARDIS's databanks. It could record the life story of this doomed moon a thousand times over and still have room to spare. But Foyo liked to *read* the notes. He liked to see them.

And so, there were stacks of pages in his library. There were stacks in the galley, and the observatory, and the swimming pool. There were times he thought that his TARDIS navigated the centuries slightly slower than it should, as if the timeship was literally weighed down by the knowledge it held.

Like you.

For a moment, the glow of the control column took on the bleached hue of sour milk, and Foyo had to look at his notes until it went away.

'Show it to me again,' he said, and let the page he was holding join the pile on the floor.

It wasn't a very important moon. No advanced life forms. No colonies or rare mineral yield. It didn't even have a name, bar whatever Foyo might record in the circular script of his people. There were far more interesting planetoids in this sector, with some real potential in the civilisations there . . . once they stopped hitting each other with rocks.

The only thing that *really* set this moon apart was that it had exploded, and, no matter how many times Foyo watched that happen, he had no idea why.

The TARDIS's engines flexed, and before him the exploding moon paused in its annihilation. Oh, Foyo *knew* time itself wasn't stopping. It was the TARDIS – stepping out of the natural flow of the universe to skip back up the timestream. But no Time Lord was immune to that little spark of arrogance that told you that the opposite was true – that the universe moved for you, and not the other way round.

Unseen machinery growled, and the moon reassembled. Continents came back together. Debris interwove. Suddenly, the planetoid was just as it had been for aeons – a bright little pebble against the brushed velvet of the void.

Maybe that was why he needed the pages. The surety of it, in a universe that was anything but sure.

'Oral notation,' he commanded, and the TARDIS began to record his words, even as the moon began to come apart again. 'Fourth observation of detonation. Total species death in under forty seconds. Have tried geological scans.

Atmospheric reads. Sentient-life audits. And yet . . . no cause can be found.'

Exploding planets were a hobby of Foyo's. He collected them. Or the data related to them, anyway – reams and reams of it, cluttering the halls and vaults of his TARDIS the way a mythical dragon might hoard gold. It wasn't *for* anything. In another life, Foyo had been a researcher at the Academy, but that was a long time ago. Now, he just collected. And tried not to wonder at what point a hobby became an obsession.

'Nothing,' he said to himself. 'It's bewildering.'

Pages blurted and rustled. A quadrillion deaths, from the microbiological to the massive, all recorded in black ink on white paper. The thought occurred to Foyo that he might have done something about it. Not prevented the explosion – he didn't know what had caused it – but saved some of the species that were going extinct in front of him. He had the space, certainly. Some of the marine organisms could have slept in the pool.

But that wasn't what Time Lords did.

'Run scans again,' Foyo said suddenly. There was something. Something wrong. Something itching at the edge of his senses. The printer buzzed again, and Foyo caught the first sheet between console and floor.

'There,' he said. 'Look.' He scrambled around the floor until he found the last set of results. 'The numbers don't match.'

Foyo Vedrashimeen was not, on the whole, a Time Lord given to panic. Some of that was the safety of the TARDIS, of course. Nothing could reach him here. Some of it was the fact that his hobby was the death of planets. If something wasn't going wrong, well, there was nothing to see.

But now . . .

'How can that be right?' he whispered. 'The death toll is different between detonations.' Foyo might not have noticed it, had the numbers not been right in front of him. 'A million or two fewer deaths,' he breathed. The buzzing of the printer had become distressingly loud, as if the TARDIS shared his unease. 'Between one detonation and the next. But that doesn't make any sense. It's the *same event*. Where did they go –'

The prickling deepened on the back of his neck, and then, like a lightning bolt, came the sting.

When Foyo regained consciousness, he was on his back. His hearts were labouring, strumming in his chest like insect wings. *Poison*, he thought blearily. *I've been poisoned.*

'A fascinating species,' came a voice. 'Unnamed, of course, like everything else on that boring little rock.'

Something feathered against Foyo's cheek, then ran over his nose. The air above him was swimming with bodies. Thousands upon thousands of bodies – segmented red and black, buzzing so loudly he could barely hear the panicked roar of his TARDIS.

'A stinging vespid,' the voice continued. 'Length of your hand. Stinger like a syringe. Nasty little thing. I say little – their swarms grow into the millions. When they do . . . well, everything runs, or everything dies. They'll eat anything.'

The voice was monstrous with glee.

'Even paper.'

Foyo forced himself upright, dislodging a whole host of insects. They stung him for it – fat spikes of agony. But they were stinging him anyway, and he wanted to *see* who had done this. To him. To his TARDIS.

The vespid things were everywhere. Crawling over the console. Burrowing into his notes. He could hear the clacking of mandibles as a million mouths chewed through his life's work. Two of the hideous insects spiralled upward, fighting over a sheet of paper. The control column was dark with a mat of heaving bodies. A horrid coughing came from above, as a great glut of vespids forced their way into the fluted mouths of the control column. He could hear his TARDIS choking. The sound was the worst thing he had ever heard – which was something, considering he watched worlds die all the time.

'Why are you doing this?' he croaked.

There was a shadow standing over him, half hidden by the blizzard of red and black. Watching dispassionately. Crawling with wasps.

'Because you watched,' they said, and then the stings came again, and again, and again.

They walk in silence.

The boy does not speak, as per tradition. The Time Lords do not speak, because there is nothing to say. Dust the colour of oxblood stains their robes. It tastes like tin, and ozone and power.

Ahead, light the colour of milk peals and crackles. It dances at the edges of the boy's sight, but he keeps his eyes on the ground.

It is not yet time for him to see.

Caratessi Thochoser didn't hear about Foyo Vedrashimeen's death. She was too busy running for her life.

It was a clear day in the Death Zone of Gallifrey. The Eating Fog had not yet come down the mountains. The anarchitects still slumbered under the scrubby grass of the plain, sleeping off their feast of Sontarans the day before. From her vantage point on a high crag, invisible behind her cloaking device, Caratessi watched a huge gorgaraptix pad cautiously towards a pool of water, unaware of the hungry nanites drifting within.

A clear day. A good day. To die, and to live, and to die again.

She had discovered this place entirely by accident. Most Time Lords believed the Death Zone to have been deactivated. Apparently it wasn't the done thing any more to scoop up the most dangerous creatures in the universe and pit them against each other for Gallifreyan amusement.

Soft, she mused. *We've gone soft.*

Now, the whole place was abandoned. A stretch of wilderness more than 6,000 kilometres square, packed with deadlier creatures and deadlier traps. All the deadlier now, of course. She was the only new arrival they'd had in centuries. Anything that still survived here had been fighting tooth and nail for its life for a very long time.

Maybe that was why she felt so fond of them.

The gorgaraptix dipped its snout to drink, and then howled as the nanites lunged forward like a tidal wave, taking the huge reptile apart molecule by molecule. Caratessi didn't stay to watch. She had other prey in mind.

There. A tiny figure, half running, half stumbling across the scrub. *Fascinating.* Caratessi was always intrigued to see how long it took her subjects to realise the danger they were in. The Death Zone was a disorientating place to wake up in at the best of times, and it was never long before its permanent residents noticed fresh meat.

Some subjects, she was proud to say, rose to the occasion. They fashioned weapons from discarded tech, struck out for the borders of the time bubble that protected this place, even ruled tiny, short-lived kingdoms from ancient ruins.

And one or two simply gave up, lying down to await their fate. Caratessi hated those most of all.

The figure fell again, gasping loud enough to bring the whole Death Zone down on their head. Caratessi sighed and lifted her rifle. *Time to motivate them properly.*

The gun was not of Gallifreyan make. She'd found this piece in the Zone itself – just a primitive hunting rifle with a steel barrel and rugged wood stock. Gallifreyan sidearms had scopes that read potential futures, painting targets on the could-be and might-have-been. All this rifle had was a simple iron sight.

It required skill. And that felt right. This was a test for Caratessi, as much as it was for her prey.

The first shot hit exactly where it was supposed to, striking a puff of dust inches from the struggling figure's ear. They flung themselves forward with admirable reflexes, looking around wildly for cover. Caratessi aimed again carefully, and the figure froze as if it could feel the unfired shot, throwing back the hood of their tattered cloak to reveal a face identical to Caratessi's own.

Caratessi Thochoser had always been obsessed with death, ever since she was a girl. Her death, and the deaths of others. It was a little taboo, a little grotty, to talk about the thrill of regeneration, but Caratessi had burned through four of her own out of sheer curiosity before she'd devised this far more . . . elegant solution.

She raised the rifle again, taking aim at the clone of herself sprinting across the plain. For a moment, just this moment, Caratessi felt a rush of affection towards them. It wasn't their fault this had happened. They were at the mercy of forces bigger than themselves, forces they would never understand, forces that would grind them up and spit them out without ever really registering their presence.

For a moment, Caratessi was a child again, and that awful unlight was pealing across her face.

She took aim at herself, and the rifle blew up in her hands.

Caratessi Thochoser did not process herself tumbling from the granite crag. She didn't register the impacts that stole her breath, or the nasty pop that might have come from her cloaking generator crunching against a rock or her ankle meeting the ground. She was too busy berating herself. She'd been lost in reminiscence. Been distracted. In the *Death Zone*.

Fool, she thought, gasping as she tried to pull herself upright and put weight on her broken leg. *Damned, damned fool*.

But she wasn't dead. She knew what dying felt like. The process of regeneration was unmistakable, and her cells didn't have that sparking sense now. She had been blindsided by something, yes, and that was so embarrassing she might hunt and kill every being in this Zone so nobody could bear witness to it, but she was still alive, and –

'Hello, Caratessi.'

The voice came from thin air, and Caratessi whirled, wielding the ruined stump of the rifle like a club. *Another cloak? Hidden transmitter?* Caratessi didn't know. It frightened her that she didn't know. It frightened her that she had been so outmanoeuvred in a place she so completely believed her own.

'Why are you doing this?' she hissed. 'What do you want from me?'

'I don't want anything,' the voice said casually. 'And you have bigger things to worry about, dear Caratessi.'

She was alone. She was unarmed. Her cloak had been destroyed. She was in a place specifically crafted to kill her.

'Bigger problems,' she whispered acidly. 'Like what?'

And then she saw them, coming over the hill. Not running, as she had seen so many of them do before. Walking. Walking towards her, slowly, as if they had all the time in the world. The weak sun caught on their scavenged daggers, the shards of metal in their hands. Their faces were her face. The unlight reminded her of . . .

'Goodbye, Caratessi,' the voice said. 'And . . . thank you.'

There are many things of which the Time Lords do not speak.

Some of this is jealousy. Even at eight years old, the boy knows that Gallifreyan supremacy is built upon secrets – the secrets of their TARDISes, the secrets of time travel, the secret weapons in their vaults and the secrets to their regeneration.

He'll know those secrets someday. He'll know all of them.

But first, this.

The caldera is a cauldron-shaped hollow, crumbled like a cavity in the mountainside. It would have been utterly unremarkable but for the throbbing unlight at its core.

The Untempered Schism. A rift in space-time. A glimpse into everything that is and was and might be. Every acolyte who wishes to join the Academy must come here. To be a Time Lord is to have stared into that abyss and, with cool disdain, the boy notices how the three Time Lords escorting him cannot bring themselves to look again.

'Now,' one of them says.

I'm special.

The boy looks.

There are many things of which the Time Lords do not speak.

Some of it is jealousy.

Some of it is fear.

Codubo is a quiet world.

Tucked away beneath the galactic plane like change in an old coat, Codubo is notable for three things and three things only – a strain of rare mineral deposits, a chain of bakeries a Peladonian food critic called 'home to the finest sausage rolls in Mutter's Spiral' and its violent, beautiful storms.

During Storm Times, the small and scattered population of Codubo engages the compact and powerful engines that winch their small domed homes underground. Tall antennae extend from the humped domes. A single lightning strike to one of these antennae will power a dome for a year.

There isn't much to do on Storm Days. Codubons stay home, or throw little parties for friends and family to distract from the hurricane winds outside. In the capital, however, some of the largest underground shopping complexes stay open, so customers can spend the nineteen-to-twenty-five-hour duration of a storm shopping to their hearts' content.

Hendor Soto loved those people. There was no danger from Storm Days any more. Not really. But there was something adventurous about trading your comfortable home for being out in the underground world when spears of lightning lashed down from heaven, shaking Codubo to its foundations. It was an illusion of adventure. But an illusion of adventure was just the right amount for Hendor and his wife.

There were twelve bakeries now, all across Codubo, but it had all started here – just a simple office stripped out by hand and filled with little wooden tables and the old stone oven. Not much had changed since then. More award certificates on the wall, certainly. Hendor wasn't prideful, but he wasn't without pride. Everything else, though – the varnished wooden counter, the little tip jar dark with age, the little painting of Hendor's mother – all of that was exactly as it had been when the place opened, thirty years ago.

The bell above the door tinkled.

'Safe Storm Day,' Hendor said, as the man approached the counter. 'What'll it be?'

'You're Hendor Soto?' the man asked, as if Hendor hadn't spoken. An outworlder by his accent (though you could also tell an outworlder by the way they twitched every time a lightning bolt pranged off the shielding thirty floors up).

This outworlder, however, did not look like the twitchy type. The black suit, the goatee, a sort of sleepy, assured hostility – Hendor found himself trying to remember whether their health-and-safety permits were up to date.

'Yes,' Hendor said. 'Can I help you?'

You spent a lot of time being unobserved in Hendor's line of work. He didn't mind that. Families came in, or couples, or people who wanted a Storm Day to themselves, and once they had ordered Hendor was very happy to let them get on with it. He was background noise. That suited him. He was, at heart, a quiet soul.

He'd never had anyone look at him as closely as this outworlder looked at him, and he did not like it one bit.

'Fascinating,' the outlander murmured. 'And you don't remember me at all?'

'Remember you?' Hendor said, still writhing under that pin-sharp gaze. 'Why would I remember you –'

And then Ella swept from the kitchen like a sunrise and kissed the air beside Hendor's cheek.

'Well, don't just look at him, Hen,' she said sweetly. 'I do apologise, sir. He's a better chef than he is a server, I do promise you.'

Her warmth broke the spell, and suddenly the outworlder was smiling too, though his voice was sharp and cold.

'Well, I do hope so,' he said. 'I've travelled a long way to find you.'

'Off-world!' Ella said, expertly setting her tray down and slipping between Hendor and the stranger to guide him to a seat. 'How very exciting. Never been, myself. I like good storms and good food, and I don't see myself finding better than here. Home is where the heart is, isn't that what they say?'

'I've always thought so,' the outworlder said, and then drew a pistol and fired.

When Hendor and Ella had first courted, she had taken him to holo-films not ten doors down from the building that would become this bakery. She liked horror, and crime, and stories with action and blood, and Hendor went to them because he liked her. And in those stories, when someone was shot it seemed like the camera took great pleasure in lingering on every moment, on exploring the collapse in distressingly deep detail.

But when Ella was shot she just fell, silent and ungraceful, and then the outworlder turned to him.

'You really don't remember me?' he said.

Hendor heaved the till at him. It was like something out of a holo-film, except that when the heroes of those stories did it, the till would sail manfully through the air and take out three criminals at once. Here, it just hit the outworlder in the knee and made him scowl in frustration, but the action gave Hendor enough time to slam his hand down on the alarm button on the countertop.

++ SECURITY SYSTEM ACTIVATED.
EJECTING ALL NON-AUTHORISED LIFE-
SIGNS ++

The teleporter had been Ella's idea. It didn't have much range, and using it drained the shop's generator down to dangerous levels, but in her words it was 'far more elegant than her having to throw a ruffian out'.

The outworlder dissolved in a flurry of pixelated light, reappearing outside the bakery with a murderous expression on his face. He aimed and fired again, but the shot dissolved against a haze of protective shielding, transparent as glass and hard as tempered steel, and before the echo of the impact died away Hendor was kneeling by Ella's side.

'Please. Please don't die.'

What a stupid thing to say.

'You idiot,' Ella whispered fondly. 'It's not really up to me.'

Another shot. The whole place rang.

'Ella, you have to get up,' Hendor hissed. 'That's a plasma carbine. The shields aren't going to hold out – you have to *get up.*'

'You know more than I thought about guns,' Ella said dreamily. 'Must be all those films.'

Her breath caught on the last word, and he reached down to check her wound. She caught his hands.

'Don't, my love. I don't want you to. To have to.' She smiled weakly. 'You know you hate blood.'

He was crying. Why wasn't she crying?

'Why is this happening? Why is he doing this?'

Another shot, denting and rippling the shields before the overworked generator straightened them out. They wouldn't last long. And that should have bothered Hendor because it meant he would die too, but he couldn't think of anything other than the sight of Ella struggling to breathe.

'You didn't have to do this!' he snarled at the man standing outside, through his tears. 'What is this – a robbery? We would have just given you whatever we had. You didn't have to hurt her!'

The outworlder didn't respond. He almost looked bored – pistol braced on his wrist, emptying round after round into the shield so it buzzed and cracked. Like he was following a recipe he already knew by heart.

'Are you sure . . .' Ella said, heaving each breath out, her exhalations oven-hot against his cheek, '. . . money is what he's after?'

He stared at her. The wavering shields had turned the sick colour of milk.

'What are you talking about?'

'I found this,' she said, and held up her hand. It took Hendor a moment to realise what she was holding.

A watch. An ornate fob watch, of a type and design he had never seen.

'I've never seen that before in my life,' he said.

'Liar!' the outworlder snarled, voice buzzy and tinny through the shield. He stormed forward and slammed his fist into the hazy light and Hendor flinched as it *bent*, distorting like the skin of a balloon under a child's thumb. Another shot. Two at most. 'You remember me. You remember me!'

The manic hunger in his voice was more terrifying than the gun.

'I swear,' Hendor said, 'Ella, I swear, I swear I don't know what he's talking about.'

The hurt in her eyes. The sorrow.

'Hendor . . . did you bring this down on us?' Ella breathed, and then died before Hendor could respond.

He stared at her body for a very long time. The outworlder was still hammering on the shield with the butt of his pistol, and the often-repaired, never-replaced generator of the bakery he and Ella had built sparked and complained. When the unlight of her eyes became too much to bear, he got to his feet – an awkward, pot-bellied old man whose heart had been cut out.

The watch was an icy weight in his hand.

'Computer,' he said. 'Shut down security protocols.'

The shields parted like fog, and the outworlder stepped back into the bakery, smoothing his suit with one hand, pistol loose in the other.

'Now,' he said, as if they were simply two businessmen resuming a meeting. 'If you could –'

Hendor threw the watch at him.

'This is what you wanted?' he shouted. The man appeared taken aback. 'This is why you took Ella from me? To steal some old antique? A device for keeping time?'

The outworlder looked down at the watch for a moment, and then idly tossed it back. Hendor caught it without thinking.

'I'm not here to steal it,' the outworlder said. 'I'm here to make you open it.'

And Hendor's fingers found the clasp.

A chameleon arch is an old Time Lord trick. A way to modify your biodata. To hide as a lesser race. A way not just to conceal your identity from the universe, but from yourself as well. Rarely used, of course, because of the pain of transformation. And the shame – so unbecoming, for a Time Lord to pretend to be lesser. To give up their identity. To abandon what made them special.

The watch opened, and light spilled out.

After every Storm Day, after the winds had died down and the lightning had dissipated and the Guild of Atmospherics had given the all-clear, there was a morning of uncanny stillness and peace. Codubons would go outside, blinking in the harsh sunlight, and try to map how their world had been utterly reshaped.

That was what Hendor felt in that moment. Memory unfolded like a storm – driving him to his knees, filling him with crackling flame. He felt purged. Annihilated. Reborn.

He was not Hendor. He was more than Hendor. Hendor was a suit he had worn, a skin he was shedding, and beneath it was a cosmic force vast in its knowledge and terrible in its rage.

A Time Lord. He was a Time Lord.

'Now do you remember me?' Ella said from behind him, and then pain lanced through him.

It wasn't a knife. The Time Lord once known as Hendor knew that instantly. It was some sort of regeneration-siphoning device – the kind of thing that would get your entire timeline erased if Gallifrey knew you possessed it. He felt it now – shutting down his cells, draining his life energy until the world greyed out at the edges.

What kind of *Time Lord* carried such a thing? What kind of Time Lord would use it against their own kind?

But then he looked at Ella standing over him, and he knew.

'We should have stopped you,' he whispered. 'Before all your many crimes. Before you could become the monster you are now. We should have locked you into the Death Zone and thrown away the key.'

He swallowed. The pain was really quite something.

'As soon as you began calling yourself the *Master*.'

'It's Missy now,' the Time Lord once known as Ella said, brushing soot from where the round had scorched the back of her dress. Some sort of energy-absorbing fabric, he guessed, though of course he never would have recognised it before. It would have broken the old baker's heart to see his beloved wife like this – standing over him with arms folded, a poisonous smirk on her face.

But neither one of them were those people any more.

'What do we do now?' the outworlder said. That cool amusement was back, but Hendor could see the madness fraying its edges, now that blood had been spilled. 'I have some ideas –'

'Course you do,' Missy said, and there was suddenly a flat little multi-tool in her hand. The outworlder didn't even have time to scream before light baked him from the inside out.

'Clones these days!' Missy said conversationally. 'I got the idea from Caratessi. It's so hard to find good help, and I did *want* to see whether you might recognise an old face of mine. But what can I say – I've never been one for sharing.'

The aftermath of a chameleon arch reset is as disorientating as it is painful. Two lives trying to fill the same body – the red skies of Gallifrey warring for space with memories of spices and recipe books.

'I don't understand,' he whispered. The pain was ebbing away, and it was no comfort at all because he knew he was ebbing away with it. 'You pretended to be someone else for *years*. Why? Just to break an old man's heart?'

'Well, you do have two of them,' Missy said. 'And I owe you. You and Caratessi and Foyo and the rest of them. All those Time Lords who walked me to that caldera. Who showed me the universe. This is me thanking you for making me who I am.'

She kneeled, smoothing out her dress.

'You remember it, don't you? The unlight of it. Shining through you. Bleaching out everything. You never forget it. It drives us. Changes us. What is it they say?'

She smiled, and it was the purest expression of hate Hendor had ever seen.

'Some run away. Some are inspired. And some go mad.'

ACKNOWLEDGEMENTS

BBC Children's books would like to thank James Goss, Vanessa Hamilton, Ross McGlinchey and Gabby De Matteis for their contributions to this book.

With thanks also to Gary Hopkins and Big Finish for their permission to include the characters of Lady Calcula and Colonel Nasgard in 'The Last of the Dals'. These characters were created by Gary Hopkins.

With thanks to Paul Magrs for permission to include the character of Iris Wildthyme in 'Velvet Hugs'. Iris Wildthyme was created by Paul Magrs.

With thanks to Elsa Dicks for permission to include the use of the Death Zone in 'Tempered'. The Death Zone was created by Terrance Dicks.

With thanks to Hannah Hatt, for permission to include Brigadier Lethbridge-Stewart in 'Velvet Hugs' and 'My Daddy Fights Monsters', and Fiona Lethbridge-Stewart in 'My Daddy Fights Monsters'. The character of Brigadier Sir Alistair Gordon Lethbridge-Stewart was created by Mervyn Haisman and Henry Lincoln.